THE DELTA & JAX
MYSTERY SERIES

"In this exciting third adventure for Delta and Jax, the young sleuths and their friends find themselves falsely accused of vandalism in the present day while also immersed in a supernatural mystery 250 years in the making. From Hilton Head and Daufuskie Islands to Lake Marion, the intrepid tweens explore the beauty and dangers of South Carolina and delve deeply into Revolutionary War history in a race against time to save past and present alike—and maybe change their future in the process. Masterful storyteller Susan Diamond Riley delivers another page-turner of a Lowcountry mystery, certain to delight readers of many ages."

—**Jonathan Haupt, coeditor of** *Our Prince of Scribes: Writers Remember Pat Conroy*

"I couldn't put this book down! Beautifully written and well researched, *The Sea Witch's Revenge* is an amazing story of two siblings, Delta and Jax, as they delve into the Revolutionary War history of the island they call home. Ghostly tales, legends, intrigue, and just the right amount of history make this a must-read for children and adults."

—**Kim Poovey, author of** *Shadows of the Moss*

"*The Sea Witch's Revenge* mixes a mad box, false accusations, and a magic diary into a brew of a story that is Susan Diamond Riley's best Delta and Jax adventure yet! When endearing characters are wrongly accused, there is drama and a quest for the truth. Riley weaves in Lowcountry history and a time warp twist that will capture readers' imaginations. In this way she offers a deeper journey into the nature of revenge and the importance of forgiveness, and a clever inspection into the nature of our histories and ourselves."

—**Elizabeth Robin, author of** *To My Dreamcatcher*

"Written for thrill-seeking, curiosity-driven readers, *The Sea Witch's Revenge* is an exciting, time-twisting adventure. When a wrong must be made right, Delta and Jax Wells are on the case. In this beautifully written mystery, the young, super-sleuth Carolina siblings investigate sinister suspects, curious clues, and harrowing history. They seek justice within their Lowcountry community of families, friends, and foes. Read on, dear reader, to experience excellence in historical fiction by Susan Diamond Riley!"

—**Lisa Anne Cullen, author-illustrator of** *Haskell & Greta: A Carolina Folktale*

"Seamlessly weaving together fact and fiction, past and present, Susan Diamond Riley's descriptive writing immerses readers in all the fun flavors and folklore of South Carolina's Sea Island coast. Join preteens Delta, Jax, and Darius as they get back on their bikes for one more adventure around Hilton Head Island. Investigating the mystery of a strange, centuries-old diary, they learn about Lowcountry history during the American Revolutionary War, while also discovering that conflict between neighboring island communities may not be a thing of the past."

—**Danielle Koehler, author-illustrator of** *The Other Forest*

"Once again, Susan Diamond Riley entertains and educates on every page! *The Sea Witch's Revenge* is a delightful mix of nonstop Hilton Head Island adventure and Lowcountry history. This is NOT just a children's book. If you love the Lowcountry, read yourself some Susan Diamond Riley!"

—**Terri Johnson, coordinator of the Coastal Discovery Museum Sea Turtle Protection Project**

"It's like meeting old friends again in the latest Lowcountry adventure with Delta and Jax. In *The Sea Witch's Revenge*, the siblings are faced with a current-day dilemma as well as a link to the past when a girl from the 1780s communicates to them through a mysterious diary. A fun, fast-paced read!"

—**Ann Lilly, author of *Scoot's Savannah Rescue***

"Susan Diamond Riley's beautifully-written tale is a magical blend of fun adventure and lowcountry lore. If you love sea turtles—like me— you'll love this book! An inspiring read for all ages!"

—**Mary Alice Monroe, *New York Times* best-selling author of the *Beach House* series**

"Buckle up for some Lowcountry adventure! *The Sea Island's Secret* is a spooky mystery seasoned with history dug straight out of the pluff mud and saltwater shore of Hilton Head Island! Tremendous fun."

—AJ Hartley, ***New York Times*** bestselling author of ***Steeplejack and Cathedrals of Glass***

"What do you get when you put together a couple of young sleuths, the remains of a skeleton, a cantankerous pirate, a Civil War secret, a possible ghost, and a head-scratching puzzle to solve? That's what you'll find in *The Sea Island's Secret*, a fast-paced and rollicking mystery that will keep you turning pages till the very end and learning some history on the way!"

—**Cassandra King Conroy, best-selling author of**
Tell Me a Story: My Life with Pat Conroy

"*The Sea Turtle's Curse* by Susan Diamond Riley is a beautifully written middle-grade book which follows the journey of Delta and Jax Wells, siblings who must unravel a mystery to break an ancient curse before their world is completely turned upside down. I found myself sitting on the edge of my seat, wanting to know what happens next, but not wanting the adventure to end. A remarkable tale that will make you laugh, cry, and cheer. A feel-good story that will delight readers of all ages."

—**Dana Ridenour, award-winning author of the** *Lexie Montgomery series*

"Young readers will enjoy this island adventure. Five stars!"

—**Children's Literature Review**

"*The Sea Island's Secret: A Delta and Jax Mystery* instantly absorbs the reader in a non-stop adventure that starts with the harrowing discovery of a skull buried in mud. Enter a ghost, to help the children find a buried treasure. The plot is expertly interwoven with

Charleston Lowcountry history, and favorite places for visitors and locals. The siblings wrangle occasionally, which makes the book even more realistic. This book is a best bet for children's historical fiction."

—**Fran Hawk, author of** *The Story of the H.L. Hunley* **and** *Queenie's Coin*

"In *The Sea Turtle's Curse*, Susan Diamond Riley takes us on another great adventure with siblings Delta and Jax and their friend Darius. Set in the South Carolina Lowcountry, this mystery intrigues, entertains, and even teaches—wonderful history, geography, culture, and heroes—without being at all teach-y, not an easy thing to pull off, and she does it perfectly. Beautifully written, fast-paced with great twists, and just plain fun, this is a book that I'm eager to share with young readers!"

—**Rebecca Bruff, award-winning author of** *Trouble the Water*

"In her debut novel for children, Susan Diamond Riley braids together an intriguing mystery, two determined young siblings, an appreciation of Civil War history, and a deep love of Hilton Head Island. The result—*The Sea Island's Secret*—will appeal to mystery lovers, history buffs of all ages, and anyone who enjoys spending time on the beautiful Carolina coast."

—**Mark I. West, editor of** *RISE: A Children's Literacy Journal* **and book review editor of** *The Children's Literature Association Quarterly*

The Sea Witch's Revenge
A Delta & Jax Mystery

by Susan Diamond Riley

Published by

◄ köehlerbooks™

3705 Shore Drive
Virginia Beach, VA 23455
800-435-4811
www.koehlerbooks.com

THE
SEA
WITCH'S
REVENGE

A Delta & Jax Mystery

SUSAN DIAMOND RILEY

VIRGINIA BEACH
CAPE CHARLES

To Damian, Hansen, and Marley—
my "new history."

Table of Contents

1

Hearing the Tale

"The islanders came for the teenage girl in the middle of the night, carrying torches just like in old monster movies. But this story is real and happened right here on Hilton Head Island."

Despite the mid-October humidity, twelve-year-old Delta Wells shivered in the gloom of the old cemetery. She was flanked by her younger brother Jax and their friend Darius, both wide-eyed as they listened to the frightening tale of a girl falsely accused more than 300 years ago. They had begged Darius' older cousin, Micah, and his friend Ivy to bring them to this creepy site for a night of spooky storytelling. In the deepening darkness, the leaning tombstones seemed to take on gruesome shapes, their carvings eroded by salt air and the ravages of time. As the group sat in a circle around a battery-powered camping lantern that Darius had brought from home, the teen storytellers were not disappointing their rapt audience.

"Until she became the Sea Witch, Constance True was just a girl like you or me, Delta," Ivy said solemnly.

"Constance *True*? So, this is a *true* story?" Jax asked, laughing at his own joke.

Delta scowled at her brother. "Shut it, Jax! You'll ruin the mood."

"As a matter of fact, this story did actually happen," Micah said.

Ivy nodded and continued her tale. "Constance grew up here on Hilton Head back in the early 1700s. After her parents died when she was just a baby, she and her grandmother lived alone in a small house by the sea. But as she grew into a teenager, the townspeople started pointing out everything about her that they felt was strange. She had wild, curly hair the color of flames, and she let it fly loose rather than wear it under a cap as was the style of the day. She didn't bother to dress in fashionable clothes, either, and sometimes had the nerve to go out in public wearing men's pants!"

"So, what's the big deal with that?"

"It's not a big deal *now*, Jax, but back in the 1700s, it was practically unheard of for proper ladies to wear anything but dresses," Ivy continued. "The townspeople were suspicious of how Constance and her granny kept to themselves, not socializing with their neighbors or even going to church on Sundays, which everyone on the island except them always did."

"Just because she was different from the others doesn't make her a witch," Delta said.

"*We* know that now," Micah said, "but the islanders back then were afraid of her differences and thought she must be up to no good."

In the dim light of Darius's lantern, Delta could see Ivy's face glow orange as she nodded.

"That's right. They noticed that she spent a lot of time collecting shells and sea plants from the beaches of the island, which she then took home to make what they called 'evil potions.'"

"Maybe she was making medicines or something," Darius suggested.

"She probably was," Ivy agreed, "but the people wanted to believe she was trouble. One morning, some local men saw her combing through the surf during a terrible storm, which they thought was especially weird. They approached her and began taunting her, calling her 'Sea Witch.' One man ripped the seaweed she had been gathering out of her hand and threw it into the ocean, while another pushed her down into the surf."

"Geez, I'd be mad if I was her," Jax said.

"She *was* mad," Ivy said. "She told those men that she hoped the sea would bring them nothing but pain. Not long after, one of those men went out fishing one day and never returned. His boat washed up empty a couple of days later."

"So she *was* a witch!"

"The islanders sure thought so! They all marched to her house in the middle of the night and carried her out kicking and screaming. When her grandmother tried to help, one of the men knocked the old woman to the ground! By the light of their torches, they dragged Constance down to the beach by her wild red hair and officially accused her of being a witch. After binding her hands and feet with ropes, they set her adrift on the waves in a small boat. As she floated away, she could be heard shouting her final curse to the people of Hilton Head: 'May the waters around this island bring you misfortune and, when they do, may you hear me laugh.'"

"Whoa," Darius muttered.

"The next morning, a local woman thought she saw Constance through the fog on the beach. Turns out it was a bright red fox combing through the seaweed, but word got around that Constance had returned in the form of a fox. For decades after that, folks around here considered a fox on the beach to be a bad omen. 'The Sea Witch is getting ready to laugh,' they'd say. And maybe she was."

"Or maybe she was just a teenage girl who dared to be herself, and got murdered for it," Darius said softly.

The group sat quietly for a moment, pondering this horrific thing that had happened on their island home so many years ago. Only the chirping of crickets and the croaking of frogs, unseen in the night, broke the silence. Darius's lantern flickered briefly before the batteries died and plunged the old cemetery into total darkness. Delta let out a small scream and, instinctively, all five kids reached for those on either side of them.

Suddenly, out of nowhere, a white light shone in the middle of their circle. Delta jumped as a disembodied voice called out to her and her friends.

"You don't belong here!" the voice declared.

2

Finding the Box

After the scare at the Zion Cemetery, the following morning started out pretty harmless. Delta and Jax were helping Pops sort through an old storage room at the Island History Museum, where he was the director. The museum building itself was actually an old house that had once been the center of a flourishing rice plantation. Up until about 150 years ago, that is. When the Union Army took control of Hilton Head early in the Civil War, all of the wealthy plantation owners had fled the island and abandoned their land—and their slaves. This property had become a regular farm for a while, before eventually being turned into a well-known site for learning about the Lowcountry's past and present. In addition to the indoor history, nature, and art exhibits, the museum boasted several acres of waterfront hiking trails, native plants and animals, a butterfly house, and classes on everything from indigo tie-dyeing to kayaking through the marsh.

Delta and Jax often spent time at this popular spot now that they were living full time with their grandparents on Hilton Head. The family had all agreed this arrangement would be best for the kids while their mom and dad spent a year tracking meteorites on the steppes of Siberia for Chicago's Field Museum of Natural History. Delta and Jax admired their parents' passion for their careers, but they did miss them sometimes. Virtual visits and phone calls helped, but internet connections in northern Russia were spotty and unreliable. Even so, Tootsie and Pops had made their grandkids feel right at home in their house on Hilton Head, and in the few months they'd been living here, Delta and Jax had made friends and grown to truly love their new island home.

The siblings had opted not to tell their grandparents about the encounter at the Zion Cemetery last night, though. Tootsie and Pops knew the teens had shared some ghostly tales, but they had assumed the storytelling happened at Darius's house. Delta and Jax had not bothered to correct that assumption.

Standing in the musty museum storage room, lit by a single flickering bulb, Delta recalled the shadowy old cemetery. The setting last night had been spectacularly creepy, and the kids had all been spooked by Ivy's tale of the Sea Witch. Then, of course, the sheriff's deputy had arrived and nearly scared them to death when he shone his flashlight in their faces.

"You kids shouldn't be hanging out here so late," he'd told them. "This site is closed after dark."

"It's alright," Delta explained. "I'm Delta Wells. My grandfather runs the Island History Museum, and he hosts events here sometimes."

"We've been doing Ghostly Tales here for the Fall Festival," Micah added.

Deputy Jones directed his light toward the teenager. "Oh, hey there, Micah," he said, recognizing the local high school's star quarterback. "The Fall Festival was yesterday. That doesn't mean you can be here after dark any old time. Y'all should get on home."

The deputy had led them all back through the maze of crumbling tombstones to the dimly lit gravel parking lot and watched as they climbed into Micah's old car. Deputy Jones followed them out onto the main road in his official sheriff's department vehicle, then turned and drove in the opposite direction. Their evening had been cut a bit short, but the deputy had barely even scolded them. So, what was the point of mentioning any of it to Tootsie or Pops?

"Whoever's box this was must have been crazy!" Jax laughed.

Crowded into the jam-packed storage room at the museum, Delta glanced over to see her brother holding a wooden chest the size of a large shoe box. Given the faded wood and rusted hinges, it must've been around for a very long time.

"Why 'crazy'?" Delta asked.

"Or angry," Jax replied, pointing to a word scratched crudely into the lid of the box. "See, it says, *MAD*."

"Weird," Delta agreed. "I wonder why anyone would have carved that there?"

"How's it going in here?" Pops called, stepping into the room. "What's that you've got there, Jackson?" Pops was the only person who ever called Jax by his full name.

"Just a crazy old box." Jax laughed, showing his grandfather the letters on the lid.

Pops took the old container and examined it closely, then opened it up and looked inside.

"Well, there's nothing in it. I don't recall ever seeing it before, but it doesn't appear to be anything of historical significance." Pops had been a history professor at the University of South Carolina before he retired and took over the museum on Hilton Head. History was kind of his thing.

"I know what we ought to do with it, though," he said. "Y'all have been leaving stuff scattered all over the house, so let's take it home as a gathering spot for whatever I find that you've neglected to put away." He winked at Delta. They both knew that Jax was the one always leaving his stuff everywhere.

"Okay, but can you take it home with you?" Delta asked. "We've got our bikes, and we told Darius we'd stop by his house for a bit." Today was no ordinary Monday. It was the beginning of a weeklong fall break from school, and the friends wanted to plan out how they would spend the free days ahead. Who knew what adventures awaited the trio?

3

Planning the Break

Delta always loved spending time at the McGee house. Darius McGee was the first friend she and Jax had made on Hilton Head this summer, and his family was as welcoming and kind as he was. His dad, Mac, was a history buff like Pops, except he specialized in the culture of his own Native American ancestry. Darius's mother, Miss Ruby, was a jolly woman, fond of hugs and trying new recipes at her family's restaurant, The Geechee Grill. She was descended from slaves who had worked cotton, rice, and indigo plantations right here on Hilton Head Island a couple hundred years ago. Darius had explained that when they were freed after the Civil War, these former slaves became known as the Gullah-Geechees. They settled their own land on the island and began to govern themselves. Delta couldn't imagine what it must have been like to be a slave, owned by someone else and forced to work for them. She wondered how Darius felt about that, but it was an awkward conversation to begin. Many Gullah families still lived on Hilton Head Island, where they continued to share the unique foods, music, art, and even language of their culture.

"Hey, y'all!" Darius waved as Delta and Jax pulled their bikes into his front yard. His house towered over them, perched on concrete stilts to avoid occasional tidal floods from the marsh on its other side. Across the lawn stood other houses, which Delta knew were homes to some of Miss Ruby's relatives. In fact, Darius's older brother lived in one cottage with his wife and five-year-old daughter, Keisha, just steps from the stilted house. Darius had told them it was Gullah tradition for the family land to be shared, and Delta and Jax loved all the people and excitement that always seemed to be happening there.

The siblings parked their bicycles and joined their friend sitting on the steep steps up to his raised front porch.

"I've got an idea for something we can do during our break this week," Darius told them. "We can go visit my pet goat."

"You have a pet goat?" Jax asked, his eyes wide.

Delta laughed. "That's so random! Why do you have a pet goat?"

"And why haven't we ever seen it?" Jax added.

"Remember, I told you about him," Darius said.

Jax shook his head. "Nope. We would definitely remember that."

Darius shrugged. "Well, I thought I'd mentioned him. Anyway, his name is Bubba, and my uncle takes care of him over on Daufuskie Island."

"Where Honey and Indy used to live?" Jax asked. Nowadays Darius's Marsh Tackies stayed on the grounds of the Island History Museum, where visitors could learn more about this local horse breed that had lived in the area since Spanish settlers brought them over in the late 1500s.

"Yep. My goat Bubba is still over there on the community farm. Uncle Rob says we can come over and see him if we want."

"How would we get there?" Delta asked. She had seen Daufuskie Island across Calibogue Sound from Harbour Town. Located on the south end of Hilton Head, the famous red and white striped lighthouse drew crowds of tourists to Harbour Town each year. The area offered a great view of Daufuskie, but Delta knew there was no bridge over to the neighboring island. "I'm not sure your little motorboat would get that far, Darius."

"Yes, it would," he replied, clearly offended, "but we'll just take the ferry over. It's about a thirty-minute ride, and we might even see dolphins along the way. Micah's friend Jon lives over there, and he and Micah help out at the farm a couple of times a month to earn community service hours for school. Micah will ride the ferry with us, and Jon said he could meet us at the boat dock with his dad's golf cart."

"Are we going to play golf there?"

"You don't even know how to play golf, Jax." Delta laughed.

"I know how to play mini golf."

"We're not playing any kind of golf there." Darius smiled. "There are hardly any cars on Daufuskie, though, so most folks drive golf carts. It'd be pretty far to walk to the farm from the dock."

"Well, I think riding a golf cart around the island sounds like a blast anyway," Delta said. "When were you thinking we would go?"

"Uncle Rob said we could come by on Friday afternoon."

"Would we be back by dinnertime?" Delta asked. "Annette Jameson invited me to her birthday sleepover for Friday night. It's the first party I've been invited to since we moved here full time, and all the girls in my class will be there. I can't wait!"

"Sure, we can make that work," Darius said. "We'll head over there right after lunch on Friday. Up until then, we can do other fun stuff."

"Other fun stuff like camping at Lake Marion?" The trio looked up to see Darius's dad descending the steps from the house. "I just got off the phone with your grandfather," he told Delta and Jax, "and we thought we'd take you three upstate to the lake on Wednesday. We can spend a couple of nights at the state park. Anybody interested?"

"I'm great at camping, Mac! I spent two whole weeks at Boy Scout camp earlier this summer!"

"Your Pops mentioned that, Jax. Anyone else?"

Delta and Darius agreed that a group camping trip sounded like an amazing way to spend part of their fall break. The weather would be cooler in the northern part of South Carolina, and they might even see some leaves already changing color.

A minivan pulled onto the property, and a woman Delta didn't recognize exited from the driver's seat and opened the side door. Darius's niece Keisha burst out and ran toward them.

"Grandpa Mac! Uncle D! Uncle D's friends! Look what I've got!"

Her pigtails still bouncing from her run across the yard, the little girl held out her tiny hand to display her treasures.

"What are those little things?" Jax asked.

"They're acorns from a live oak tree," Darius told him.

"It must've been a baby tree then. Live oaks are huge!"

"Not necessarily," Mac said. "That breed of tree just has small seeds. It's like the old saying, 'Mighty oaks from little acorns grow.'"

"They're from the giant tree by my friend Maria's house. We gathered them during our playdate," Keisha said. "I brought enough so we can all plant them and grow our own beautiful forest." She handed several acorns each to Mac, Darius, Delta, and Jax, who dropped his in the pocket of his cargo shorts.

"Gee, thanks, Keisha," Delta said, discreetly waiting until the little girl had run upstairs to the house before following Darius's example and tossing her tiny acorns across the yard. "This place is about to get way more wooded!" She laughed.

As Maria's mom pulled her van back onto the street, she almost collided head-on with a sheriff's department vehicle turning into the driveway.

"Fancy meeting you here!" Mac said as Sheriff Thompson parked and got out of his car. The sheriff nodded at him without a smile.

"Hello, Mac," he said. "Is your nephew Micah around by any chance?

"I believe he's out back fishing," Mac said. "D, why don't you go get him? Is the sheriff's department involved in that scholarship Micah's getting?"

"No, I'm afraid I've not come about any scholarship."

Delta and Jax still sat on the steps, waiting through the awkward silence until Darius returned from the side of the house with his cousin.

"Hey, Sheriff," Micah said, extending a hand to shake. "What's up?"

Sheriff Thompson shook the young man's hand solemnly. "I understand you and some friends were at Zion Cemetery last night."

"That's right," Micah told him. "We were just telling some ghost stories, like we did for the Fall Festival the night before."

"We were all there," Jax said, motioning to Delta and Darius.

"I told the deputy it was okay because my Pops runs the Island History Museum," Delta added.

The sheriff turned to Delta and Jax. "Oh, so you're the Wells kids. I suppose it's good I caught you all together then."

"What's this about, Sheriff?" Mac asked, no longer smiling.

"It seems that early this morning, after your little 'storytelling' session, a caretaker over at Zion discovered that someone had vandalized the cemetery—tombstones knocked over, graffiti painted on the side of the mausoleum. It's a real mess over there."

"Wow! It was dark by the time we got there last night, so we didn't even notice anything messed up when we were there," Micah said.

The other kids all shook their heads in agreement. They hadn't noticed anything amiss either.

"It wasn't like that when you arrived," the sheriff said. "The caretaker left yesterday just before dark, and everything was fine. This damage happened last night."

Suddenly it occurred to the kids that they were being accused.

"All we did was listen to ghost stories!" Delta said. "We didn't do any damage—honest!"

"She's right, sir," Micah said. "We just walked in, sat down, and then left when the deputy asked us to. Someone else must've come to the cemetery last night after we left."

Sheriff Thompson shook his head. "I don't see how that could have happened, Micah. There are security cameras in the parking lot and, aside from the deputy's, yours was the only car in that lot last night."

"Maybe they weren't driving a car," Jax suggested. "Maybe they walked in."

"We thought of that," the sheriff said, "but they would have had to walk past the cameras to get through the gate. The fence is too high to climb. Plus, I'm afraid there's some other evidence that points directly to you, Micah."

Sheriff Thompson held out his phone to show something to Micah and Mac. Delta, Jax, and Darius leaned in as well and saw a photo of the historic old stone mausoleum, built more than 200 years ago. Across its side, in florescent orange paint, was scrawled, "IHS Sharks"—and Micah's initials.

"Your football team is the Sharks, correct?" the sheriff asked. "And you're the team quarterback, and these are your initials?"

"Well, yes," Micah sputtered. "But I didn't paint that! I mean, why would I be so stupid as to put my own name on something like that?"

"That's right, Sheriff!" Mac said. "Micah is one of this island's most upstanding youth, and he's much too smart to incriminate himself that way. It looks to me like he's being set up."

The sheriff shook his head again. "I don't want to believe you did this, Micah. I really don't. But so far, all evidence is pointing to you, son. These other kids are all underage, and we don't have anything directly tying to them, but you're eighteen now and considered an adult. We'll be investigating further before any arrests are made, but it's not looking good."

Mac took Micah back to his own house across the property after the sheriff left, presumably to break the news to Micah's mom. Delta, Jax, and Darius sat forlornly on the steps.

"I can't believe they think Micah would do any of that!" Darius said. "The local Veterans of Foreign Wars post is about to give him a Good Citizen scholarship because he's such a great kid!"

"I bet they won't give it to him if he's arrested!" Jax said.

Delta felt terrible. It was bad enough that her friend was being accused of something she knew he didn't do. It was even worse that he could lose his scholarship over it. What made her feel the worst, though, was knowing that the only reason Micah was even at the Zion Cemetery last night was because she, Jax, and Darius had begged him to go there. It had all started innocently enough at Saturday night's Fall Festival.

4

Manning the Table

Two nights earlier . . .

"Gross! Goblin guts!" Keisha squealed as she jerked her dripping hand out of the black cauldron.

"Ooh, let me try!" her friend Maria cried, shoving her small fist into the same ominous container.

The two kindergartners giggled as they tested the contents of each plastic pot displayed on the cobweb-draped table. Pops had convinced his grandkids to host the "touch table" at this year's Fall Festival. Although the Island History Museum sponsored this event every year, Delta and Jax had never actually been on the island in October before. Since they were living with Tootsie and Pops for the whole school year now, they had both been excited to experience the fun they had heard so much about over the years. Of course, they had hoped to be a part of the teen- and adult-oriented "Ghostly Tales" portion of the festival at the old Zion Cemetery, but Pops had insisted that he needed them on-site at the museum. That was where younger kids and their families came for games, a petting zoo, a magic show, and lots of free candy and other refreshments.

Still disappointed about missing out on the spooky stories at the cemetery, Delta was trying to make the most of the evening. She stood behind the table, sporting safety goggles and a white lab coat bearing the name tag "Dr. I.M. Nutz." Assisting her mad scientist persona were Jax and Darius, both dressed as experiments gone wrong. Before them sat a half-dozen plastic cauldron-shaped trick-or-treat pails, each containing some innocent item that might be mistaken for something like werewolf hair or a vampire heart. Small superheroes, princesses, tigers, and more crowded the touch table to see what gruesome ingredients the mad scientist had on display.

"This is so lame!" a loud voice proclaimed.

Delta looked up to see an un-costumed boy about her age approaching her. After shoving past two seven-year-olds who had been patiently awaiting their turn, the kid thrust his hand into a plastic cauldron and laughed.

"Oh, sure! 'Eye of newt.' That's just a bucket of blueberries." He pulled out a handful of berries and tossed them in his mouth. "And those 'goblin guts' are probably just cooked spaghetti."

"No, they're not!" Jax said. "They're the pumpkin innards from our jack-o-lanterns!"

"Jax! You'll ruin the fun!" Delta shoved her brother's arm. Around them, a crowd of children stood and stared.

"What are you even supposed to be?" the boy asked Jax with a sneer. "You're just wearing a gray hoody."

"I'm half-human, half-shark, if you must know," Jax said, turning around to show the gathering crowd the fake shark fin attached to the back of his sweatshirt. He spun back around, showing the plastic shark teeth that he had just placed in his mouth. "I too ow ta tee to I coo ee ca-ee."

"Huh?"

Jax removed the slobbery piece of plastic from his mouth. "I said,

I took out the teeth earlier because I wanted to eat some candy."

"What a loser!" the heckler announced loudly.

"Have you been on the hayride yet?" asked Darius, clad in the wings, antennae, and googly-eyed glasses of a fly-man. "Maybe you'd like that better."

"Nah, this whole place is lame."

"Oh, yeah?" Jax said. "If this is all so lame, then what are you even doing here?"

The boy's face reddened. "I'm only here because I'm babysitting my little sister. My mom made me bring her to this stupid festival."

Little Maria, Keisha's friend, stepped forward with her hands on her hips. "You are not my babysitter, Enzo! Mommy isn't giving you money or anything. She just dropped us off here because she has a date tonight."

At that, Enzo grabbed his sister by the hand and pulled her toward a face-painting booth across the room.

"Don't mind those silly boys," Delta said to the group of children still standing near the touch table. "Who wants to check out the magical ingredients we mad scientists need to perform our experiments?"

As a pair of rainbow-colored unicorns approached the table and tentatively reached into a cauldron labelled "witches' fingers," Delta turned to Darius. "That Enzo always drives me crazy," she said softly.

Darius, nodded. "Yeah, he's trouble for sure."

"You guys KNOW him?" Jax asked.

"Yeah, he's in my math class," Delta whispered. "He's always sassing the teacher and bullying other kids. We've only been in school for a couple of months, and Mr. Lee has already given him detention at least four times."

"He's the loser!" Jax said, rolling his eyes.

"He used to be an okay kid," Darius said quietly. "We were in Cub Scouts together in elementary school. His dad was even our den leader.

Enzo wasn't so bad then."

A commotion at the door of the museum drew the trio's attention to a group of teenagers laughing and talking as they entered. Micah was dressed as a pirate, complete with an eye patch and a hoop earring. His friend Ivy wore a flowing white gown, her hair powdered white and her face pale with dark circles under her eyes. Their buddy Jon sported an old military uniform, with a painted gunshot wound covering most of his chest. All three wore matching sports jackets that said "Island High School Football" across the back. When the trio noticed Darius, Delta, and Jax at the touch table, they waved and approached.

"Hey, D! How goes the touch table?"

"Okay, I guess," Darius replied with a shrug. "The little kids like it, anyway."

"How was Ghostly Tales at the cemetery?" Delta asked.

"*Omigosh*, it was amazing!" Ivy said, as Micah and Jon both nodded enthusiastically. "We each had a spooky story to tell about someone who had died on the island. I'm the ghost of the Sea Witch." She spun in a circle, allowing her long dress to swirl around her.

"And I represent Captain Pope," Micah said, removing his tricornered pirate hat as he bent into a deep bow.

"My guy got shot with a musket during the Revolutionary War!" Jon announced proudly.

"You guys all look great!" Delta told them.

"Yeah," Darius agreed. "We should take a picture of y'all in your costumes." He pulled out his cellphone and the trio of teens threw their arms around each other and grinned for the camera.

"Wait!" Delta said. "We need a pic of you without your coats. They ruin the effect."

Micah, Ivy, and Jon all slipped out of their football jackets and dropped them in a pile on the museum floor. This time they each made a scary face as Darius snapped their photo.

"Oh, y'all are terrifying." The group turned to see another teen wearing an identical football jacket.

"Hey, Waldo," Micah said, although Delta didn't think he sounded especially happy to see his teammate.

"You're Waldo?" Jax said. "Everybody's been looking for you!" He looked toward Delta and Darius. "Get it? Like in those *Where's Waldo?* books."

The teen just rolled his eyes, his arms crossed over his chest. "Hilarious. Like I haven't heard that a couple of thousand times."

"It's a nickname, Jax," Darius whispered. "His last name is Wallace, and you don't want to mess with him."

"I didn't expect to see you here," Jon said to his teammate.

Waldo shrugged. "I'm picking up my sister. She's doing the face painting." Delta saw a dark-haired young woman across the room packing art supplies into a plastic toolbox. "Let me know if you need any tips on kicking," he directed to Ivy. "You don't want to embarrass yourself out there, you know, since you're representing our whole school."

Delta recalled hearing that Ivy had recently been chosen as kicker for the Island High football team—the first female to have that honor in the school's history.

"Thanks, but I think I'll do just fine," Ivy told Waldo. "I hope there won't be any hard feelings about me replacing you, though. I mean, Coach judged us fair and square."

Waldo's face turned red. "Yeah, right. All he cared about was good press for the team. Bragging about having a girl kicker and all that."

"Ivy is an awesome athlete," Micah said, "but Coach would have replaced you no matter what. You've skipped practices, your grades are going downhill, and you're lucky to even be on the team at all."

"Thanks for your input, Oh Perfect One." Waldo turned and stomped toward the face-painting booth and his sister.

"Why, there's my soon-to-be-famous nephew—the athlete, scholar, and all-around good citizen!"

Ruby, Darius's mom, rushed into the room and embraced Micah in a bear hug. Dressed as a scarecrow in a floppy hat and patched denim overalls, a smiling Tootsie followed close behind her, along with a tall, blonde woman whom Delta didn't recognize. Turning to the blonde woman, Ruby continued her bragging. "This is who I was telling you about! Micah just found out he's being awarded the Good Citizen scholarship from the VFW on Veteran's Day. A full-ride to any state university in South Carolina!"

"What wonderful news!" Tootsie said. "And much deserved."

"Congratulations, Micah. That's something to be proud of, for sure," Ruby's other friend said. "I'm Councilwoman Taylor, from the Hilton Head City Council."

Micah blushed as he thanked her, and then put his arm around Jon's shoulder. "My buddy Jon is getting an award, too."

The women turned their attention to Jon, who smiled and shrugged. "Just an award. No scholarship money involved."

"Well, congratulations to you, too, Jon," Tootsie said. "Money or not, it's a great honor."

Ruby put her hands on her hips, eyeing the teenagers' ghoulish costumes. "You three look mighty spooky tonight! How did storytelling go at the cemetery?"

"At the cemetery?" the councilwoman asked, suddenly looking concerned.

"We told historic tales at the Zion Cemetery," Ivy explained. "Everybody seemed to love it!"

"You had crowds of people tromping through that historic site in the dark?" Councilwoman Taylor was frowning now, looking nothing like the friendly lady who had congratulated Micah just moments before.

"Well, yes, ma'am," Micah stuttered. "The museum set everything up. We were just volunteering our time to help . . ."

"Hmph!" With her arms crossed over her chest, the councilwoman turned and marched toward the museum lobby, where Delta knew Pops was saying goodnight to the evening's visitors.

"Don't mind her," Tootsie said. "She's just very protective of the historic sites on the island. She doesn't want anyone messing them up, but then I don't suppose any of us do!"

Delta could hear the councilwoman's raised voice coming from the lobby, where it sounded like she was scolding Pops.

"Anyway, I'm glad y'all had fun tonight," Ruby continued. "Darius, let me know when you're ready to head home."

With the crowds mostly gone, Delta, Jax, and Darius began clearing their touch table. They stacked the lightweight plastic cauldrons into a large cardboard box they'd hidden underneath the table. They could clean out the contents once they got them back to Tootsie and Pops's house.

"I still wish we could've been at the cemetery with you guys," Jax said to Micah. "It sounded so cool, and we missed the whole thing."

Suddenly, Delta had a great idea! "Hey, guys! Maybe we could go out there some other time and you could tell us the stories, just us!"

"I don't know," Micah said.

"Aw, c'mon, Micah!" Darius begged. "Please! What harm could it do?"

"Yeah," Delta chimed in. "It's basically what you did tonight, except with way fewer people."

"We could do it tomorrow night, while you still remember the stories," Jax said.

"I guess we could," Ivy said, looking at Micah. "What do you think?"

Micah hesitated, and then shrugged. "Sure, why not? You in, Jon?"

"'Fraid not," Jon said. "I've got family stuff tomorrow night. But y'all have a blast."

"Can I come?" a voice called from across the room.

Delta looked up to see Enzo approaching. She thought he'd left already.

"Sorry," Jax said. "This is a private event. Only friends and family."

Enzo frowned, and then laughed. "I was just kidding anyway. Who'd want to hang out with you losers?"

"You're right about that, little dude," Waldo added, accompanying his sister toward the museum lobby. "You kiddies have fun in the spooky graveyard tomorrow night."

"We *will* have fun!" Delta said. "I can't wait!"

Now, just two days later, Delta was wishing she'd never suggested that private storytelling session in the first place. She'd gotten Micah in major trouble, and she had a feeling things were only going to get worse.

5

Getting the Blame

"Do you think Tootsie and Pops will kick us out and make us go live in Siberia?" Jax asked his sister the next morning.

"Why would you even ask that? Everyone agreed that it was best for us to live here while Mom and Dad did their work thing over there." The duo was sitting on the wooden dock at the edge of their grandparents' backyard. The narrow freshwater canal it overlooked was only about twenty feet across—nothing like the broad marsh visible from Darius's house. The siblings sometimes kayaked on this waterway, but never swam there. The dock was a great place to watch alligators, turtles, and the myriad birds that called this area home. For Delta and Jax, it was their go-to private talking spot.

"Yeah, but when Tootsie and Pops agreed to let us live here, we weren't criminals," Jax sighed.

"We're not criminals now, goofwad! We didn't do any of that damage at the cemetery."

"*We* know we didn't do it, but we're still being accused of it." Jax suddenly jumped up. "It's just like the Sea Witch! She was accused and punished whether she was guilty or not. In fact, maybe she's to blame for all of this. She didn't like that we were telling stories about her in the cemetery the other night, so now she's getting her revenge!"

Delta rolled her eyes. Her brother could be so dramatic at times. "The Sea Witch didn't spray-paint graffiti on the mausoleum, Jax. I just don't want Tootsie and Pops to think that *we* did it."

"Or Mom and Dad!" Jax added. "What if they decide that living here with Tootsie and Pops isn't working out after all, and they make us come live with them in Siberia! They don't even have Wi-Fi there most of the time, Delta!"

She had no response to that. What if Jax was right, and this cemetery mess ended up changing everything for them? Hilton Head Island was just starting to feel like home. Mom and Dad would be so disappointed in them, just like she feared Tootsie and Pops felt.

Apparently, Sheriff Thompson had headed to the Island History Museum yesterday right after he left Darius's house. He had told Pops everything and had given him quite a scolding for allowing the kids to go there after dark—which, actually, he had not done. Delta and Jax had spent the evening defending themselves to their grandparents.

"Honest! We were just there listening to ghost stories!" they had insisted.

"I agree it doesn't sound like anything I'd expect from you two," Pops had said, shaking his head. "But you and your crew sure seem to be the likely suspects."

Tootsie hadn't said much, but she looked like she might cry during the whole conversation. That was worse than any punishment.

"Are you going to tell Mom and Dad?"

"I would if I could, Delta," Pops had said.

Ouch! Pops always called her his pet name: Delta-Boo.

"Your folks said they'd be out of internet and phone range for the next week or so," Tootsie had said, "so we'll just have to wait until the next time they're able to call. Hopefully this whole thing will be cleared up by then."

But this morning, the situation had gotten even worse. Councilwoman Taylor had called Pops to say that she was officially recommending that the Island History Museum no longer be allowed to host events at historical sites on the island. She said Pops had abused the privilege by giving his grandchildren permission to be there after hours. That meant the upcoming Veterans Day celebration, where Micah was supposed to receive his scholarship, might not even happen. But then, Micah might not even get his award now at all. What a mess!

"Hey, y'all. Your grandma said you were back here."

Delta looked up from her seat on the dock to see Darius strolling across the yard toward them. He plopped onto the wooden surface next to her and heaved a heavy sigh.

"All hell's breaking loose at my house," he said.

"Yeah," Jax said, "Pops is in trouble with that councilwoman, too. She says the museum can't be trusted because Pops let us go to the cemetery."

"Except he *didn't*," Delta added. "And how did she even find out about the vandalism? Do you think the sheriff told her?"

Darius shrugged. "Maybe, but there's an article about it in today's newspaper. She might have seen that. I mean, it doesn't include the names of any suspects or anything, but she could have gotten that from the internet."

"What do you mean?" Delta asked.

"You remember that football guy, Waldo? His sister was doing face painting at the festival the other night."

Jax nodded. "Oh, yeah. He was kind of a jerk."

"You could say that," Darius agreed. "He made a post on that 'Island Neighbor' social app about the mess at Zion, saying that this year's star quarterback and 'Good Citizen' wasn't such a good citizen after all. He didn't mention Micah's name, but anyone could figure it out. Plus, he said the community should boycott the Geechee Grill in protest. Hardly anyone was there for breakfast this morning. My parents are really upset."

"Oh, man, Darius! I'm so sorry!" Delta knew that the restaurant had been in Darius's family for generations. It was a local favorite, serving traditional Gullah dishes like shrimp gumbo, fried okra, and sweet potato pie. Just thinking about it was making Delta hungry. Anytime she had been at the Grill, it had been packed. Diners usually had to wait outside for a free table. But apparently, not today, not since Waldo's post.

"Well, mostly old people follow that app," Jax said. "Like parents and grandparents. Not everyone will see it."

As if on cue, a whistling sound emanated from Delta's pocket. She reached in and pulled out her cell phone, and then furrowed her brow as she read the screen.

"You guys are not going to believe this," she said. "Enzo just sent this message to our entire math class: 'Spread the word! My mom just heard from the Island Neighbor that some students at our school did a lot of damage at the Zion Cemetery the other night. That's messed up! Just because you're related to or friends with the guy who runs the Island History Museum, that doesn't give you the right to be a juvenile delinquent!'"

Delta looked up, her face pale. "Everyone will know he's talking about us!"

"This is the worst fall break ever," Jax said.

6

Discovering the Diary

After Tootsie had served them a lunch of ham sandwiches and potato salad, the kids were still feeling no better. Midway through their meal, Delta had received a text from Annette Jameson uninviting her to the Friday night sleepover: "My parents said I need to cut my guest list. Not enough room in our house for everyone. Sorry!"

Delta had seen photos of Annette's enormous home and knew there was more than enough room for their entire grade to attend.

"Maybe we can get together some other time," Delta had texted back, but Annette never replied.

"She saw Enzo's message," Delta said, straining to hold back tears.

"Not necessarily," Jax told her, munching on his sandwich. "Maybe her parents saw the Island Neighbor post."

Delta groaned. Unless she and the others cleared their names, none of the island parents would want their kids hanging out with any of them. They would be social outcasts for sure.

The kids were putting their plates in the dishwasher when Pops stuck his head in the kitchen.

"By the way, I put that new box of yours to use last night. One of you left a pile of acorns on the end table in the living room." He stared right at Jax.

Delta had forgotten all about the old wooden box they'd found at the museum. She vaguely recalled Jax absentmindedly emptying the pockets of his cargo shorts last night during their tense discussion. Pops must have found the gift that Keisha had given them from her friend's live oak tree.

"C'mon, Darius," she said. "Come see this cool old box we found." The trio headed into the living room, where Jax lifted their discovery from the coffee table.

"I call it the 'Crazy Box', because somebody carved *MAD* on it," Jax said, pointing out the letters on the lid. "Get it? Because *mad* is another word for *crazy*."

He lifted the lid and turned to Pops. "Where'd you get the book?"

"What book?" Pops asked.

"There's a little book in here with the acorns," Jax told him.

"I just put in the acorns," Pops said, halfway out the front door. His lunchbreak over, it was time for him to head back to the museum for the afternoon. "Maybe Tootsie added the book. Honey, did you put anything in the kids' box?"

"No," she called from the kitchen. "I didn't even know they had a box!"

"Huh," Pops said. "I think you kiddos are playing a trick on us."

Kiddos. That was a good sign. Maybe he wasn't so upset anymore.

As her grandfather left the house, Delta examined the odd volume that had mysteriously appeared in the Crazy Box. Bound in faded, cracked leather, the yellowed pages were sewn into the binding with thread. "Hey!" she said, holding the book open to a particular page near the beginning. "There's something written here! Can you read cursive, Darius?"

Darius nodded and took the book. He pushed his glasses up on his nose and squinted as he examined the ornate script on the unlined page.

"Whoa! This is really old!" he said. "The date written here is 17 October 1781. It says:

> Dear Guardian Angel,
>
> I turned eleven years old today, and Papa gave me this new journal in which to document my thoughts. I suspect he also believes the extra practice will improve my penmanship.
>
> My first thought as I write is that my brother will not respect my privacy! He placed more than a dozen acorns in my special box last night—the one Papa made for me last summer from that fallen branch of our neighbor's magnificent tree. I carved my initials into the top of the box to show that it is entirely my own, and my intent is to keep my journal safely stored inside it. I wish Jamie would just leave it alone, but at least he is still too young to read and, therefore, cannot know what I write to you.
>
> Oh, Guardian Angel! I nearly forgot to tell the most exciting news! Our neighbor, Mrs. Talbird (whose tree provided the wood for my special box), arrived at our home just before sunset last evening. Her husband is up north fighting honorably with Marion's Men, and she needed my mother's help. You see, Mrs. Talbird delivered a baby son early this morning, so we shall share a birthday! I believe he will be called Henry.
>
> Your devoted, MAD

Darius looked up from the page to find Delta and Jax staring at him in confusion. Jax spoke for all of them. "What the heck?"

"How did that get in our box?" Delta asked. "It was definitely empty when we found it, and Tootsie and Pops were the only other people who had access to it. They said they didn't put it in there, and they wouldn't lie to us about it. I mean, why would they?"

"And how did that kid know about my acorns?" Jax added. He quickly counted the nuts in the box. "Yep, exactly thirteen. 'More than a dozen'—just like it said."

Delta shook her head in disbelief. "That is so weird."

"Well," Darius said, "at least you know now why the box has *MAD* carved on it. It's somebody's initials. I wonder who 'MAD' is. Or *was*, I should say."

Delta pulled her cell phone from her pocket and tapped something onto it. "I just did a search on 'Talbird, Hilton Head' and found this: 'Talbird Plantation, on the banks of Skull Creek. Owner, John Talbird. Bequeathed to Henry (Yorktown) Talbird. Plantation house burned by Loyalist unit in 1781; rebuilt after Revolutionary War.'"

"Hey! That new baby ends up owning a whole plantation!" Jax said. "But what's the 'Yorktown' part about?"

Delta shrugged. "I don't know. That's all it says."

The trio sat in silence for a moment, each wondering about the old journal and its mysterious arrival. Finally, Jax spoke.

"But really, how did MAD know about those acorns? It's too big of a coincidence that some little kid almost 250 years ago put exactly the same thing in that box that Pops did. And then that diary shows up out of nowhere. I'm gonna test it."

"What do you mean?" Darius asked. "Test it how?"

Jax disappeared down the hallway into his bedroom and returned shortly clutching something in his fist. He opened his palm to show the others what he held.

"Pops gave me some old toy soldiers from an antique shop. I'm going to put one of them in the box and see if MAD notices." He laid the toy inside and motioned for Darius to replace the journal as well.

"You don't think that kid is actually writing to you from the *past*, do you?" Darius asked. "That's crazy!"

Delta shrugged and smiled. "Who knows? After all, it *is* the Crazy Box!"

7

Reading the Past

Delta and Jax had never pedaled so fast. The morning sun was still low in the sky when they skidded into Darius's front yard and dropped their bikes in the gravel driveway. Delta was just stopping to prop hers up on its kickstand when a voice called from nearby.

"Y'all need to move those bikes onto the grass, please." Darius's mom was sticking her head out of the driver's side window of her minivan. "I've got to get to the Grill, for all the good it'll do me. Yesterday was so empty in there, all you could hear was crickets chirping."

"Sorry, Miss Ruby." The siblings hurried to move their bicycles out of the van's path.

"You've got bugs at your restaurant?" Jax asked.

"No, sweetie," Ruby replied with a bit of a smile. "That's just an old saying. It's just that news travels fast on this island, and that trouble at the cemetery is hurting our business."

"You know we didn't do any of that damage, don't you, Miss Ruby? And Micah didn't, either. I swear it!"

"Oh, you don't have to go swearing, Delta," Darius's mother

replied. "I know y'all are good kids. Rumors are powerful things, though, and until the sheriff finds the real culprit, y'all seem to be getting the blame. It's not fair, is it?"

"No, ma'am, it's sure not," Delta said. She and her brother had been away from Chicago for less than six months, and yet, Delta was already starting to speak like a Southerner. Darius often called adults *sir* or *ma'am*, and apparently it was starting to rub off on his friends.

"Darius was finishing breakfast when I came downstairs," Ruby called as she pulled out of the driveway. "Y'all go on up."

Delta and Jax trudged up the steep steps to their friend's house, the morning's initial excitement dampened a bit. "Do you think the sheriff is even *looking* for the real culprit?" Jax asked. "What if he's just searching for evidence to prove *we* did it?"

"Then he won't find anything, will he?" Delta replied. "Because we *didn't*." She tapped on the screen door at the top of the staircase. "Hello . . . it's us! You in there, Darius?"

"I'm on the porch," Darius called. "Come on back."

Delta and Jax entered the house, savoring the aroma of bacon and waffles. They passed through the homey living room, furnished with comfy couches and filled with family photos, and headed out to the screened back porch that spanned the length of the house.

As it did every time, Delta's heart quickened when she took in the view. Live oak trees, dripping with Spanish moss, framed the scene on either side. Stretching out beyond them was the glistening Intracoastal Waterway. Studded here and there with fields of swaying spartina grass, golden in the October morning light, the marshy shoreline was home to egrets, herons, crabs, and more. Farther from land, islets of oyster beds protruded from the lapping waves, and Delta could see a beached boat on one bed. Nearby, two harvesters collected the mollusks in large pails. Someone would be eating fresh oysters today.

Darius stood by the screen, looking down at something in the backyard. As Delta approached, she followed her friend's gaze and saw Micah slumped in an Adirondack chair by the stone firepit. The teen looked miserable, sitting by himself, staring into the unlit coals.

"How's Micah doing?" Delta asked.

"Not too good," Darius replied. "A man from the VFW called last night and said Micah should prepare himself. They won't give him the Good Citizen scholarship if the sheriff arrests him for the cemetery mess. The man said they might not give it to him anyway, just because of all the bad press it's generated."

"That's so unfair!" Delta said. "What happened to 'innocent until proven guilty'?"

Darius shrugged. "The few people who've come into the Grill while Micah was working there kept staring at him and whispering, so Mama told him to take the rest of the week off to just chill."

"Maybe he can hang out with Jon and Ivy," Jax suggested. "They always have fun together. I bet they'd cheer him up."

"He might see Jon, but Ivy's parents hit the roof! Her older sister got into some kind of trouble a few years ago, and now her mom and dad assume the worst about Ivy, too. She's grounded for, like, the rest of the school year or something, and she's not even guilty."

"I feel like this whole problem is our fault," Delta said. "We practically forced them to take us to the cemetery that night."

Darius nodded. "I feel terrible, too. You know, my aunt doesn't have the money to send Micah to college without that scholarship. He's been trying to figure out who could have set him up like that, but so far, he's come up with nothing. Especially since the cameras all show that we were the only ones there."

Delta scowled, deep in thought. They just had to figure out the truth of what happened that night at Zion Cemetery in order to clear all of their names.

"So, anyway, what's up? I didn't think I'd see y'all until we went

THE SEA WITCH'S REVENGE

camping this afternoon."

Darius's comment brought Delta back to their reason for visiting him so early. "*Omigosh!*" she said. "You'll never believe it!"

Jax grinned as he took off his backpack, unzipped it, and pulled out the Crazy Box. "Guess what we found in here this morning?"

"A handful of acorns and a tiny soldier?"

"Yes," Jax said. "Plus, a brand-new message from MAD that just happens to mention my little gift."

"No. Way." Darius's mouth hung open in amazement.

"Yes, way," Jax said. He lifted the lid of the box and waved the old journal in front of Darius's face. "My experiment proved successful!"

"We're not that great at reading cursive," Delta said, "but we could read the words *toy soldier*. Somehow that kid knew Jax put it in the box!"

Jax handed his friend the book. "Can you read the whole thing for us?"

Darius opened the journal and flipped to the entry they'd read yesterday. Turning the page, he found a new message. "This is so weird. This definitely was not here yesterday, but the paper and the ink is old—like, really old."

"What does it say, Darius?" Delta asked, and her friend began reading aloud.

18 October 1781

Dear Guardian Angel,

Jamie continues to place items in my special box—this time, a toy soldier. I confronted him about it, and he swears he has never put anything in there, but who else would have done such a thing? Mother says I must be a good sister and get along with Jamie, so I have decided to view these trinkets as gifts to me, since they are in my box.

"So, MAD is a girl!"
"Shush, Jax. Let him read."

Mrs. Talbird is feeling much better today and even allowed me to hold baby Henry! He is a funny little thing, wrinkled and bald like an old man. Mother says I should not mention that to Mrs. Talbird, as she believes her son is beautiful.

Mother also told me that Mrs. Talbird and Henry will be staying with us at Two Oaks for some time. I later overheard Mother tell Papa that Mrs. Talbird has no home to return to! It seems that the Tories from Daufuskie paid an unwanted visit to our island two days ago. Mother says the Sea Witch must be laughing, because the Tories stole up by boat and burned every plantation house on Skull Creek, including Mrs. Talbird's!

Apparently, one of Mrs. Talbird's slaves saw the troop advancing and warned her. She bade her slaves to hide in the woods, and she bravely stood her ground at her house until the men arrived. The strangest thing, though, is that the Tory in charge of the attack turned out to be Mrs. Talbird's very own brother-in-law, Philip Martinangel!

Mrs. Talbird told Mother that Captain Martinangel took pity on her (given that she was his wife's sister and about to give birth). He instructed his men to enter the home and carry out all of its contents and place them a safe distance from the house. They did so, placing all of the furniture, silver, clothing, bedding, etcetera beneath the Talbird's giant oak tree (from whence came my box!).

THE SEA WITCH'S REVENGE

Captain Martinangel told them, "I was charged with burning every Loyalist's house on Skull Creek, but no one said anything about their belongings."

As Mrs. Talbird's husband is off fighting with Marion's Men, Papa took some of his own militia to the Talbird Oak (which they are all calling it now) and gathered the family's belongings to store until Mr. Talbird's safe return. I am happy to have Mrs. Talbird stay with us, but I do hope little Henry will stop his crying when I am trying to sleep at night.

Your ever faithful, MAD

"Mrs. Talbird's oak tree! That's where I got your acorns!"

Delta, Jax, and Darius looked up to see that Keisha had joined them on the screened porch.

"Did you plant your acorns, Uncle D?"

"Um, sure, Keisha," Darius responded.

Delta smiled, recalling clearly how the two of them had tossed their tiny acorns across the McGee's front lawn.

"That same tree is still alive?" Jax asked. "Where is it?"

"I told you the other day, silly," Keisha replied, rolling her eyes. "It's by my friend Maria's yard. We play house under it all the time."

"Oh, yeah," Darius said. "I know that tree. It's been around since before the Revolutionary War. It's huge."

"So, you're saying that the acorns Pops put in the Crazy Box are from the exact same tree the box was made from?" Jax asked. "Remember, MAD said her dad built it out of a fallen branch from the Talbird Oak."

"What are the chances of that?" Delta said. "It's like the past and the present came together."

Darius nodded slowly. "And now they're existing at the same time."

Keisha wandered back inside the house as the three older kids stared at the new diary entry and came to the same conclusion. Delta said it out loud.

"We're actually communicating with a girl from nearly 250 years ago!"

8

Investigating the Oak

"Last one there's a rotten egg!" Darius shouted as the three friends took off on their bikes toward the Talbird Oak.

They were all curious to see the old tree that had apparently connected them with the past. Although the oak was only a couple of miles from Darius's house, their route took them past marshlands, traditional Gullah homesteads, a golf course, and fancy neighborhoods filled with expensive mansions. Hilton Head had a little bit of everything.

Delta had always loved the island's leisure paths. Created for walkers and cyclers, these paved trails paralleled roads all over the island, providing safe travel options for tourists and locals alike. Vacationers often rented bicycles while they were here, and during the summer, these paths were filled with cheery bands of cyclists. Now that it was mid-October, though, Delta, Jax, and Darius had this particular trail nearly to themselves.

The trio passed a bustling seafood restaurant and entered a residential community. Orange and yellow potted mums sat on front porches strung with garlands of artificial autumn-colored leaves. Most of the living plants throughout the island were still lush and green, with palm fronds swaying in the warm breeze. Aside from residents' intentional decorations, the only natural sign that fall had arrived was the occasional crepe myrtle tree beginning to change color and the golden spartina grass in the marsh that abutted the neighborhood.

"Hey, did you guys notice that Maddy mentioned the Sea Witch?" Jax asked as they followed Darius down a side street.

"Maddy?"

"Yeah, now that we know she's a girl, I'm calling her that instead of MAD. She said her mom thought the Sea Witch must be laughing because of those attacks on the plantation houses."

"Oh, that's right," Darius said. "I noticed it when I was reading the entry, but then forgot with all the other excitement."

"I guess there was some truth to Ivy's scary story, then," Delta said. "I mean, not that the girl was really a witch, but now we know that the legend was something the islanders talked about back then. Maybe Constance True really was accused of being a witch, and really was killed by her neighbors."

"Maybe the Sea Witch is laughing now, too, about the troubles we're having."

"No, Jax," Darius said. "Her curse has to do with the waters around the island. She's only said to laugh when the trouble is water-related, remember? Like ships sinking or hurricanes blowing in from the sea."

"Or soldiers from Daufuskie sneaking up Skull Creek and burning houses?" Jax asked.

Darius nodded. "Exactly."

"She'd have no reason to be laughing at our problems," Delta said, "but I bet she would understand how rotten and frustrated we feel. We're being accused of something we didn't do, just like she was."

"You're right," Jax agreed. "And she knows all about wanting revenge for it, too."

Darius looked between Jax and Delta. "We're not after revenge, are we, y'all?"

"I am," Jax said. "I want whoever really caused all the trouble to get caught and clear our names!"

"That's not revenge, exactly," Delta said. "We're not out to punish anybody that doesn't deserve it. We just want justice—for the guilty person to pay the consequences for what they did."

"And for us *not* to," Jax added.

Darius pulled his bike to a stop in front of a mass of leaves. "Here she is—the Talbird Oak."

Delta always felt there was something magical about giant old live oak trees, so prevalent in the Carolina Lowcountry. This one filled nearly an acre of land, its massive twisting branches hanging so low that its trunk was completely hidden. The kids ducked their heads and passed through to the dark central shade. Delta could see why Keisha and her friend would love playing here.

The ground beneath them was covered with tiny fallen leaves that provided a cushioned surface surrounding a trunk the size of Delta's bedroom. She knew the leaves must be from seasons past, as the branches above were still filled with dark-green foliage. Pops had explained that live oaks got their name because, unlike the northern oak trees Delta and Jax had seen in Chicago, live oak branches were never bare. Their leaves stuck around until new ones grew and pushed them off.

"Like growing new teeth," Pops had said, "except that live oaks get new 'teeth' every year!"

Delta breathed in the musty odor of the dried leaves beneath her feet, as well as the fresh scent of the living plant above. *Past and present in one place*, she thought, *just like the acorns and wood of the Crazy Box.*

"This is the exact spot where the Tories put all of Mrs. Talbird's possessions," Darius said.

Delta envisioned the ground covered with furniture, clothing, and household goods. She shivered in the warm air as she imagined how Mrs. Talbird must have felt watching her belongings saved while awaiting the burning of her home.

"What does 'Tory' mean, anyway?" Jax asked.

"We learned about that in American history last week," Delta said. "During the Revolutionary War, the Tories were colonists who sided with the British. Some people called them Loyalists because they wanted the American colonies to remain loyal to the King of England rather than become an independent country."

Jax scowled. "But I thought that war was the British against the Americans. You mean, some of the Americans wanted to stay British?"

"That's right," Darius added. "Around here, the folks on Hilton Head were Patriots—they wanted to become the United States of America. But the people on Daufuskie Island were all Tories. Some family members were fighting on opposite sides of the war, like the Talbirds and her sister."

Delta nodded. "Because the guy who burned her house was her own brother-in-law." The trio stood reverently beneath the tree, each lost in thoughts of the events that had happened so long ago on this very spot. Events that Maddy had just written about last night.

"What are you losers doing in my yard? I didn't say you could be here!" The kids looked up to see Enzo ducking beneath the branches. He stood with his hands on his hips, staring at the trio near the tree trunk.

"This isn't your yard, Enzo," Darius told him. "The Talbird Oak is on common area owned by your neighborhood. Anyone can be here."

"Well, your bikes are in my yard, so I guess they're mine now," Enzo said. "Thanks. I was wanting a new one. And I guess I'll just sell the other two . . ."

"You're not taking our bikes, Enzo!" Delta said. "We'll move them. We didn't know they were parked in your yard." Delta, Jax, and Darius left the shade of the tree and gathered their bicycles, moving them closer to the famed oak.

"Did you know Enzo lived here?" Delta whispered to Darius.

"Yeah, I thought you knew. Keisha told you the tree was right by Maria's house."

Delta had completely forgotten that Maria and Enzo were siblings.

"Are y'all hiding from the law over here?" Enzo sneered. "I don't blame you for not wanting to show your faces in public after what you did."

"We didn't do anything!" Jax shouted. "There's no law against listening to ghost stories! Somebody else messed with the tombstones— not us!"

Enzo crossed his arms over his chest. "That's not what the whole town's saying. News is, y'all are guilty as sin."

"That's just an internet rumor," Darius said.

"And one *you* helped spread," Delta added. "You told our entire math class that we were vandals!"

Enzo shrugged. "Not just the math class. I sent that message to all of my classes. I figured they deserved to know the truth."

Delta groaned. "But it's *not* the truth!"

"Hey, don't be mad at me!" Enzo said. "That football player Waldo started it by posting on the Island Neighbor app. If you've got a problem with the news leaking out, talk to him." Enzo headed across the lawn and into his house, leaving Delta, Jax, and Darius steaming near the Talbird Oak.

"That kid makes me so mad!" Jax said, his jaw clenched. "It's like he *wants* us to be in trouble!"

"Let's just get out of here," Darius said.

"Wait!" Delta had strolled over to a historic marker sign attached to a post not far from the Talbird Oak. "This tells the story about the burning and saving the furniture and all that, but listen to this. The whole thing was about revenge."

"Huh?"

"Pay attention, Jax. The Patriots of Hilton Head killed a Tory from Daufuskie. To get even, the Tories sailed up Skull Creek and burned Patriot plantations. This sign says, 'The Skull Creek attack resulted in an escalating exchange of bloody retaliatory assaults, culminating in the deadly Muster House ambush in which nearly the entire Hilton Head militia was killed.'"

"Whoa," Darius said. "So almost all the local soldiers end up dead? That's terrible."

"At least Mrs. Talbird's husband is away fighting somewhere else, so maybe he's okay."

"I hope he is," Delta said, adopting her brother's verb tense as if the past were present. "But guess who's a member of the Hilton Head militia?"

The three spoke in unison: "Maddy's dad."

9

Setting Up Camp

It was a several-hour drive from Hilton Head to Lake Marion, so the sun was quickly descending by the time Mac's SUV pulled into the state park. The group quickly found their assigned campsite and got to work setting up the McGees's family-sized tent.

"This is different from the ones we had at Boy Scout camp," Jax said, struggling to slide a flexible pole through a tube of fabric on the tent's side. "Our tents were canvas covers over wooden platforms. They were already set up when we got there."

"Here, let me show you," Darius said, maneuvering the pole as if he had been camping dozens of times—which he had. Darius knew how to do lots of stuff, especially when it came to the outdoors, but he was never a show-off. That was one of the things Delta admired most about her friend.

"See," Darius said. "Then you bend the pole and stick it in this metal hole down here at the bottom of the tent." Suddenly, the pile of nylon became three-dimensional and began to look like an actual shelter. With Mac and Pops working on the opposite end, the tent was soon fully pitched and covered by a sort of tarp called a rain fly.

"Just in case," Mac had said. "The weather report is clear for the next couple of days, but you never know."

"No need to jinx it," Pops said, laughing. "If we *don't* put up the fly, it'll rain on us for sure!"

The kids carried sleeping bags and duffels into the spacious tent, then joined the men outside just as the sun was setting.

"We'd better gather some wood for the fire before it gets any darker," Darius said, and led the others in collecting dry sticks and fallen branches from the surrounding forest. In the fading light, they could just make out the reds, oranges, and yellows of sugar maples, sweet gums, and beech trees native to this part of the state.

"I love the plants on Hilton Head," Delta said, "but it sure is fun seeing leaves starting to change color. I guess we're just far enough north for that to happen, huh?"

Jax nodded. "Yeah, back home in Chicago, the trees are probably completely colored by now. That's way up north."

Delta sighed. Usually these days, she *did* consider Hilton Head Island and her grandparents' house "home." Her room was cozy, she'd made new friends, and Tootsie and Pops were always welcoming. Even so, sometimes she got lonesome for her old Chicago neighborhood, her school friends there, or the great selection of museums and stores in that major city. Mostly, though, she missed Mom and Dad. She knew their jobs across the world were important and only temporary. They would be back to visit in a few weeks for the winter holidays, and then home for good by this time next year. She'd found it easiest to avoid feeling lonesome for them by keeping busy, and right now, picking up firewood was just the trick.

With enough wood collected to last for several days, Darius and Jax set to work building a fire within the metal ring in their campsite intended just for that purpose. The boys propped several 18-inch-long branches upright in a tepee shape, then stuffed smaller sticks and pine needles in the cavity beneath it. Jax carefully lit the kindling with a long match, and soon the flames had reached the branches and taken hold. Within minutes, the group was sitting in folding chairs around a roaring campfire.

"Wow, Jax! I'm impressed!" Delta said. "You really *did* learn something at Boy Scout camp."

Her brother shrugged. "Told you. I learned lots of stuff."

After a simple meal of roasted hotdogs and baked beans right out of the can, the group made s'mores over the fire. As they debated the ideal shade of brown for a toasted marshmallow, the wind rustled the forest around them. An owl hooted somewhere in the darkness.

"Y'all want to tell some ghost stories?" Mac asked.

Delta, Jax, and Darius looked at each other in the glowing light from the fire.

"That's a hard *no*," Darius said. An awkward silence followed. Their last ghost story session had definitely not ended well.

"We've got a big day planned for tomorrow," Pops said, quickly changing the subject. "We can go hiking, do some fishing, and maybe rent some canoes. How does that sound?"

Everyone agreed that those options would be fun.

"Is it okay if we kids go ahead and get in our sleeping bags?" Jax asked. "We should probably get a good sleep."

Delta looked suspiciously at her brother. He never wanted to go to bed early.

"Sure," Pops said. "Mac and I will join you after a while. Just sleep in the sweats you have on. It'll get cool tonight."

Jax was first in line entering the tent. He immediately tripped over a duffel and landed in a heap on the floor, with Delta and Darius barely avoiding landing on top of him.

"Let me turn on my lantern so we can see where we're going," Darius said. He had been sure to replace the batteries before leaving home. The kids each wriggled into their sleeping bags and sat in a circle around the lantern, the bags pulled up around their chests.

Jax giggled. "If Tootsie was here, she'd have made us go brush our teeth before we went to bed."

Delta knew that was true. She rubbed her tongue over her teeth and felt the stickiness of toasted marshmallow. She really should go down the path to the bathhouse and brush them.

"So why were you so anxious to go to bed?" Darius asked Jax. "You don't seem that tired now."

Jax reached into the duffel on the floor beside him and pulled out the Crazy Box. "I wanted to talk more about Maddy's diary. We had to keep quiet about it the whole ride here." He lifted the diary from the worn oaken box and opened it again to the latest entry. "What's the deal with 'Dear Guardian Angel'?"

Delta shrugged. "I guess that's just some old-fashioned style of writing in a journal. It kind of makes sense. I mean, who are you really writing to when you write 'Dear Diary'? At least with 'Guardian Angel' she's imagining an actual *being* that's receiving her message."

Darius chuckled. "It'd blow her mind if she knew who was actually receiving it!"

"And when!" Delta added.

Jax held the book near the lantern and pointed to a spot on the page. "This part is interesting. She says one of Mrs. Talbird's slaves warned her about the attack, and then Mrs. Talbird told all her slaves to go hide in the woods. That was brave of her, to face the soldiers alone."

"Maybe," Darius said. "But slaves were valuable property then. She probably didn't want the Tories to steal them."

"Steal them?" Delta said, scowling. "That sounds so terrible when you put it that way. Like they were objects."

Darius sighed. "That's the way it was back then. Slaves were often treated like objects, and they were worth a lot of money."

"Does that make you feel weird, since your mom's ancestors were slaves?" Jax asked.

"Jax!" Delta slammed her knuckle into her brother's thigh.

"It's okay. He can ask," Darius said. "It *is* weird, and I feel lots of different ways about it. I mean, it makes me sad to think that some of my ancestors were stolen from their homes and their families and brought to a strange new place where they didn't even speak the language. And they were forced to work for somebody who maybe abused them . . ."

The three kids sat silently, imagining.

"Then, sometimes, I get really mad," Darius continued. "How could people allow something so cruel to happen? For a long time, it was perfectly legal to buy and own slaves, and since they were your property, you could treat them however you wanted."

"That is *so* wrong," Delta said.

"I'm glad it's not legal now," Jax added.

Darius nodded. "Yeah, but most of the time, I feel really proud. I mean, my mom's great-great-grandfather was enslaved here, but then he fought with the Union Army so all slaves could be free. He opened his own store on the island after the Civil War, and he worked until he had enough money to buy the land where he used to pick cotton as a slave. That's the land my family lives on now."

"That's pretty cool how it turned out," Jax said.

"You know, our mom's parents came to the United States on a boat from Cuba when they were little kids," Delta said, "but I guess their families at least had a choice. They escaped because their country was at war, but if it had been safer there, they may have stayed in Cuba forever."

"But if they'd done that, we may never have been born!"

"See? That's what I'm saying, Jax," Darius said. "If some of my ancestors hadn't come over from Africa and become slaves on Hilton

Head, I wouldn't be who I am or where I am today. Neither would my mom, or my aunts and uncles or cousins. Our Gullah culture is just part of us, and I'm proud of that. My mamaw used to say, 'Our family may not have come here by choice, but we can each choose to live our best life every day, wherever we are.'"

"That's good advice," Delta said.

Darius sighed. "Anyway, it is what it is, and you can't change history."

"Sometimes I wish we could," Jax said.

"Do you think Maddy's family owned slaves?" Delta asked.

Darius considered this possibility. "Probably. Most of the white people on the island were plantation owners at that time, and I'm guessing Mrs. Talbird would have gone to another plantation like hers for safety. Maddy said something about 'Two Oaks,' so maybe that's the name of her family's plantation."

"Why didn't the Tories burn Maddy's house down, too?" Jax asked.

"Maybe it wasn't on Skull Creek," Delta suggested. "The diary said the Tories were supposed to burn every plantation house *along Skull Creek*."

Darius nodded. "That's true. Maybe Maddy lived more inland. I wish we knew her last name, and then we could try to find out more about her and her family."

"One thing we do know is that her dad fought with the local militia," Delta said. "That would mean Hilton Head's soldiers—the ones that all ended up killed at the Muster House, whatever that was."

"Maybe it was just a yellow house?" Jax suggested.

"It's not '*mustard*,' like the condiment," Darius said. "It's 'Muster House'—m-u-s-t-e-r. Maybe it's somebody's name. Like it was their house, and their last name was 'Muster.'"

Delta pulled out her cell phone and punched in some letters. "Let's see what we can find out about 'Muster House, Hilton Head.'" After a pause, she looked up at the boys and sighed. "Exactly nothing. I've got no internet connection here."

"That's not always a bad thing," her brother said. "Let's hope Mom and Dad stay out of internet range until we get out of trouble for the cemetery thing."

Delta sighed. "I just hope the truth comes out before we have to go back to school on Monday and face everyone thinking the worst of us."

"That's only going to happen if they catch the real vandal," Darius said, "and I'm not even sure the sheriff is looking for anyone besides us."

"Then we'll figure it out ourselves," Jax said. "Who had motive and opportunity? That's what they always say on cop shows."

"Hmm," Darius said. "That's a good question. Whoever messed with those tombstones didn't just knock stuff over. They painted graffiti on the mausoleum to make it look like we did it. Who would want to get us in trouble?"

"Enzo's been enjoying this mess a little too much," Delta said. "He spread that rumor about us all over school, and he was really nasty this morning when we saw him by the Talbird Oak."

"And he was there at the Fall Festival when we were making plans to go to the cemetery. Remember, he asked if he could come along," Darius said.

Jax nodded. "Yeah, and he was mad when we told him no."

The kids sat quietly for a moment, pondering their suspicions.

"What opportunity did he have to do it, though?" Delta finally asked. "I mean, he knew we were going to be there, but how did he get to the cemetery and do all that damage without anyone seeing him?"

"He doesn't strike me as all that smart," Jax added.

"We'll have to keep thinking about it," Darius told them.

"We may not know how he did it yet," Jax said, "but that jerk is not going to get away with framing us! Not while we're on the case!"

10

Meeting the Captain

The sun was just beginning to peek through the trees when Delta awoke to someone shaking her shoulder.

"We got another message from Maddy!" Jax whispered. "Meet me outside!"

Delta rubbed her eyes and yawned. The sound of Jax slowly unzipping the tent flap was nearly drowned by Pops' and Mac's snoring. Sliding out of her sleeping bag, Delta slipped into her tennis shoes and followed her brother outside. Darius was already slumped in a camp chair.

"So, exactly why do we need to get up so early?" Darius yawned.

"Because I want to show you Maddy's message in private, before Pops and Mac get up," Jax whispered. "They'd think we're loony if we told them we're getting letters from hundreds of years ago!"

Delta had to agree it sounded unlikely, but even so, it was happening.

Jax pulled a small flashlight from his pocket and shone it on a page in the old journal—a new entry penned with fresh ink. "You read it to us, Darius."

"Y'all really should learn to read cursive," Darius said, but he took the book in hand and began to read.

19 October 1781

My dear GA,

"For *Guardian Angel*," Jax whispered, but Delta shushed him.

What excitement we had here earlier! Jamie came running to say that a horseman was coming up the drive, and who should be visiting Two Oaks but Captain Marion himself! Of course, Papa invited him in, and Mother rushed to see that he was served food and drink.

After exchanging pleasantries, Captain Marion said he had actually come to the island to see Mrs. Talbird! Discovering her plantation burned to the ground, he was naturally frightened for the lady's safety. But then one of her slaves told the captain that she had retreated to our home in time to give birth to baby Henry.

Captain Marion said he had a jumble of good news and bad news to share, so I will tell it in that order. First, the good news is that the Patriots, led by General Greene and aided by Marion's Men, have defeated the Tories at Eutaw Springs! He said they pushed the British all the way to Charleston. This happened some weeks ago, but this is the first we are hearing of it here on the island. Papa was made so happy by the Patriots' success that he whooped and hollered right there in the drawing room!

But now, dear GA, I must share the bad news, which, thankfully, is not as bad as it could be. As you know, Mr. Talbird had been fighting up north with Captain Marion for the past several months. The captain rode all the way here to personally check on Mrs. Talbird (as he knew she was with child), and to tell her that her husband was captured by those evil Tories at Eutaw Springs! They have taken him (and others) to Charleston with them, where he is imprisoned on a ship in Charleston Harbor.

Mother shook her head and said the Sea Witch is laughing yet again, but Captain Marion said not to fret. He assured us that the Patriots also captured some Tories during the battle and intend to trade those men for our own being held in Charleston. He said Mr. Talbird fought bravely and that we should count our blessings that he is still alive and, God willing, may soon come home to meet his new son. That brought Mrs. Talbird to tears, although I do not know whether they were tears of joy as her husband lives, or sadness because his home has been destroyed.

Captain Marion expressed his confidence that the Patriots will soon be victorious not just in a singular battle, but in the war itself. When that happens, America will be its very own country. Can you imagine? And yet, I cannot help but worry for Papa. I am proud of his dedication to our local militia, but what if he were taken prisoner by the Tories just like poor Mr. Talbird? I do pray that this horrid war will end soon!

I found no gift in my box from Jamie today. I suppose he has lost interest in teasing me since I no longer complain about it to Mother.

Your ever faithful, MAD

"Utah Springs?" Jax whispered. "I thought Utah was way out west somewhere. I didn't know the Revolutionary War was fought out there, too."

"It wasn't," Delta said, confused.

"No, it's not 'Utah' like the state. It's spelled E-u-t-a-w," Darius said. "If they pushed the Tories to Charleston, where Talbird was held, I'm guessing Eutaw Springs must be somewhere in the Carolinas."

"Wow! So, Mr. Talbird is a prisoner of war!" Delta said. "Do you suppose he made it back to Hilton Head eventually?"

Before either of the boys could reply, movement in the tent alerted the trio that the adults were rising for the day. Jax grabbed the old book from Darius and stuffed it under his sweatshirt.

"You kiddos sure are up with the sun!" Pops said, joining the group sitting around the fire ring. Last night's embers were cold and damp from where Mac had tossed a bucket of water on the dwindling blaze before going to bed. "Let's get a fire going so I can make us some flapjacks."

As Darius and Jax showed off their fire-building skills, Delta helped her grandfather gather the breakfast supplies. Watching him ladle pancake batter onto a hot cast-iron skillet, she couldn't stop thinking of the journal entry. Who was this Captain Marion guy? Maddy acted like it was a big deal that he had come to visit, but maybe her family just didn't get a lot of company since they lived on an island. Perhaps *any* visitor was a big deal. And poor Mr. Talbird had been taken as a prisoner, just when he was becoming a father.

Learning about the problems these people had endured centuries ago on Hilton Head was almost enough to make Delta forget the troubles her own family and friends were facing since their night in the cemetery. Almost.

11

Spotting the Battle

"Ooh! How about this one?"

Delta cringed as her brother dangled a slimy, wiggling night crawler just inches from her face. She slapped his hand away with a shudder. "Stop it, Jax! You're such a pest sometimes."

Pops and Mac were taking way too long picking out bait. The kids were eager to start fishing on the lake, but the two men were in a deep conversation with the clerk at the bait shop.

"Panfish have been biting on redworms lately," the clerk said, "or if you're angling for catfish, how about some stink bait?"

"That sounds awesome!" Jax said. "The stinkier, the better!"

Delta rolled her eyes. The shop smelled of fish and dirt, and the constant chirp of caged crickets and drone of tank pumps was starting to get to her. "Pops, can Darius and I please wait outside until you're done?"

"If you stay right out front," Pops replied. "Don't go wandering off."

The two friends headed to the parking lot, where Delta inhaled deeply. Even though the state park was only a few hours from Hilton Head, it felt much farther north. While the island still held traces of summer, with days warm and flowers in bloom, autumn had arrived here. Sugar maples had begun to turn red, and the cool air held the scent of dried leaves.

Darius must have been thinking the same thing. "Is this what fall is like in Chicago?" he asked.

Delta laughed. "Maybe on a freakishly warm day. By this late in October, we were usually wearing winter coats and mittens. There was an ice storm one Halloween, and I remember coming home from trick or treating with my costume covered in a sheet of ice!"

Darius's eyes widened. "No way! But you still went out, even in that weather?"

"Of course," Delta said. "We weren't going to miss out on all of that candy!"

A rusty pickup truck pulled into the parking lot and the two kids watched as a couple of teenage boys climbed out and headed toward the bait shop. One took the last drag off a cigarette before flicking it to the ground. Delta and Darius stepped away from the door.

"'Sup?" one of the boys asked them as he passed. The other, sporting an armful of tattoos, nodded to them as they stepped aside. As the teens entered the store, Delta heard cheerful greetings between them and the clerk.

"Teenagers always get such a bad rap," Darius said. "Those guys seemed kind of sketchy, but it looks like they just want to go fishing like we do."

"Yeah, and then there's the not-sketchy kids, like Micah and Ivy and us. People are assuming the worst about us, too."

Delta and Darius had strolled to the end of the building and turned to head back toward the door. After all, they'd promised Pops they wouldn't wander off. But as they spun, they couldn't believe what they saw on the other side of the bait shop: the Battle of Eutaw Springs!

The scene spread out before them. In the distance was a two-story farmhouse. Stretching across the front of the home, a single row of several hundred British and Loyalist soldiers stood anxious to fight for their cause. Facing them, nearly a thousand Patriot soldiers massed in groups, their bayonets held at the ready.

"No way!" Darius said. "We were just reading about this battle in Maddy's journal this morning."

With "The Battle of Eutaw Springs, September 8, 1781" painted in bold lettering across the top, the mural covered the entire side of the bait shop building.

"Look—there's a metal plaque over here," Delta said. "It says this was the last major Revolutionary War battle in South Carolina. General Nathanael Greene's American troops attacked British forces camped at an area plantation."

"The journal mentioned a General Greene," Darius said, joining her by the plaque. "This says more than five hundred Americans died in the battle, but the British lost almost seven hundred. They basically gave up and moved back to Charleston, leaving most of South Carolina in American control."

"But look at this, Darius!" Delta jabbed her finger at a line on the sign. "'The American army was composed of regular troops as well as militia, including General Francis Marion's Brigade.' That must be 'Marion's Men' that Maddy keeps talking about!"

"Well, there you are! What'd you find?" Pops, Mac, and Jax turned the corner and appeared carrying what looked to be cardboard Chinese food containers.

"We picked redworms," Jax said, waving a container.

"Hey, Pops, have you ever heard of a guy named Francis Marion?"

Mac and Pops looked at each other with raised eyebrows and laughed.

"I should say so!" Pops said. "Who do you think the lake's named after?"

It hadn't even registered in Delta's mind that they were at Lake

Marion. "So, who is he?"

Pops smiled. "Well, he *was* one of the trickiest militia leaders of the Revolutionary War."

"What's 'militia' mean, anyway?" Jax asked.

"Most soldiers were full-time, paid members of the American Army, but the militia was made up of ordinary farmers and laborers who fought part-time."

"Like volunteers?" Delta asked.

Macs nodded. "Yep. They did it for the cause, not for the money."

"Francis Marion led a militia here in South Carolina," Pops explained. "He and his men specialized in knowing the ins and outs of the area's swamps. They'd make sneak attacks on British units, and then escape into the swamp where the British couldn't follow."

"Why couldn't they follow?" Jax asked.

"For a couple of reasons," Mac replied. "First of all, they didn't know their way around these parts like the locals did."

"That makes sense," Darius said.

"But mainly, they just didn't know how to maneuver a swamp," Mac continued. "Marion's militia rode Marsh Tackies, because that breed of horse knew how to handle the terrain. The British horses refused to even try."

"Like Indy and Honey, Darius!" Jax said. The McGees kept their pair of Marsh Tackies at the Island History Museum so visitors could appreciate this unique South Carolina breed.

"So, Francis Marion was kind of famous?" Delta asked.

"Absolutely!" Pops replied. "There've been books, movies, even a TV show about him—but I suppose that was before your time. So, you've really never heard of the Swamp Fox?"

Delta and Jax shook their heads, but Darius spoke up. "Is that what they called him, the Swamp Fox?"

Pops nodded. "One British colonel called him 'the old fox' because he would appear and disappear so easily, just like a sly fox. Marion didn't actually become widely known as the Swamp Fox, though, until about a hundred years later."

"So, he never even knew that was his nickname," Jax said. "Maybe somebody will give me a cool name like that a hundred years from now."

"I could think of a few names for you right now, Marsh Rat," Delta said with a smile, slugging her brother playfully on the shoulder.

The gang climbed back into Mac's SUV and headed toward the lake.

Lake Marion, Delta thought as they bumped down a dirt road through the woods. A lake named after the guy who Maddy just said was sitting in her own drawing room on Hilton Head Island—a guy famous for sneaking up on people and then disappearing. Delta had just been kidding when she called her brother a marsh rat, but there was a sneaky rat somewhere on Hilton Head who had gotten them and their friends in big trouble. Was it really Enzo, or some other villain? Either way, how had they managed to appear and disappear at the Zion Cemetery without being seen? Maybe the Swamp Fox had the answers.

12

Climbing the Mound

Fishing turned out to be a fiasco.

Mac had parked the SUV at a clearing about a mile from the lakeshore and they'd all hiked the remaining distance to the water. Lake Marion stretched out before them, smooth as glass in the sparkling fall sunlight. A wide-winged osprey circled above them as they sorted the fishing rods on the bank.

"Who brought the bait?" Mac asked.

Everyone—including Pops—looked eagerly from one to the other of their companions. No one appeared to have the cardboard container of worms.

"I'll go back and get it," Darius said, taking off at a jog back down the long trail to the car.

"Hey, Pops," Delta called. "What was the name of this lake before they called it Lake Marion?"

"Funny you should ask. This lake actually didn't exist at all when Francis Marion was alive. The Santee River just ran through here until the 1940s. Then they dammed the river and created this lake."

"And named it after the Swamp Fox."

"That's right, Jackson. Today, it's the biggest lake in the state."

"Isn't that weird?" Delta said. "The biggest lake in the state didn't exist at all a hundred years ago."

"Sure, it did. It just wasn't this lake," Jax said. "Get it? Some other lake was the biggest one before Lake Marion came along."

Delta rolled her eyes.

"I read somewhere that Francis Marion's home—the one he lived in after the war—is at the bottom of the lake," Mac said.

"It sunk?" Jax asked.

"No, goofwad. It got covered up by water when they built the lake. Right, Pops?"

"Exactly, Delta-boo. So, do you kiddos remember how to put your hooks on the line?" They fished often off the little dock in their grandparents' backyard, but those lines were usually already hooked and just sitting in the garage ready to use.

"I could use some help," Delta admitted. "I'm not sure I remember how to tie the knot the right way."

"How about you, Jackson?"

"I'm good," Jax insisted, his tongue sticking out the side of his mouth as he concentrated on his hook. "Remember, I got my Fishing badge at Boy Scout camp last summer. I'm a pro!"

Pops smiled and gave Delta a wink. Jax never let them forget about the badges he'd earned at camp. It was amazing how much he claimed to have perfected in just two weeks.

By the time Darius finally returned with the forgotten bait, the rest of their crew had rods and reels ready to go. They each threaded a plump redworm onto their hooks, spread out along the bank, and cast their lines into the quiet lake.

"Hey, Pops! What kind of fish do you think we're gonna catch?" Jax shouted.

Pops put a finger to his lips and then pointed to the water. He had taught his grandkids from an early age that staying quiet was the first rule of fishing. After all, you didn't want to scare away your catch.

Fifteen minutes passed uneventfully. Then, Delta was reeling her line back in when she suddenly encountered resistance. "I think I got one, Pops!" she whispered.

"You know what to do. Just reel it on in, nice and slow."

Delta turned the crank and lifted the tip of her rod high, just as Pops had taught her. Little by little, she could see the line coming closer to the lake's edge. Lowering the rod, she turned the reel again, lifting its tip as she did so. Finally, the end of the line was within her sight. Holding her rod firmly in one hand, she reached out and grabbed the taut fishing line with the other. Then she lifted her heavy catch from the murky water.

Jax burst out laughing.

"You caught a big stick. That'll make a tasty lunch!"

"Shut up, Jax," Delta muttered, untangling the tree branch from her fishhook and tossing it back with a splash.

"Both of you, hush," Pops whispered.

Darius, who actually was an accomplished fisherman, scowled at his friends.

A half-hour later, Mac began to reel in a silver-striped bass more than a foot long. He might have landed it, too, if his fishing line hadn't snapped just as he reached for it. The relieved fish slapped its tail on the water's surface with a loud smack as it swam to safety.

"Doggonit!" Mac muttered, searching in his tackle box for a new hook.

Distracted by the runaway bass, Jax turned the wrong way just as he swung his arm back to cast his line.

"Hey!" Pops yelled.

Delta watched as Jax's line flew back over the lake and landed in the water with a splat—Pops's favorite fishing hat hooked firmly to the end.

"I bet Jax couldn't have done that if he'd tried," Darius said, all thought of silence abandoned for the moment. Everyone except Pops laughed. He didn't seem to find the situation humorous.

"You reel that right back in, young man," he said. "I've had that lucky hat for over twenty years."

"It doesn't seem so lucky today," Jax muttered under his breath. He retrieved the sopping hat and tossed it to his grandfather.

"Why don't you kids hike over to the Indian mound while Mac and I fish a while longer," Pops said. "It's just a short way up that path over there."

"But I want to fish!" Darius protested.

"Come on. A hike will be fun," Delta said. "You can fish at home."

Darius shrugged and placed his rod near his dad's tackle box. Delta and Jax laid theirs on the ground near Pops, and the trio headed down the lakeside path.

"So much for catching our own lunch," Darius said.

The kids emerged from the woods edging the lakefront and found themselves in a broad meadow filled with swaying grasses speckled with wild daisies and purple passionflowers. Dragonflies and orange butterflies flitted across the field as if dancing in air.

"Whoa! Look at that!" Jax pointed to a pyramid-shaped hill as tall as the nearby forest. In the otherwise flat meadow, this knoll seemed oddly out of place. "It must be the Indian mound Pops mentioned."

"Native American mound," Delta corrected. She knew Darius's paternal grandmother was from the Catawba tribe, making him one-quarter Native American. She wouldn't want to hurt his feelings.

Darius just shrugged. "Whatever. That sounds so awkward. Let's take a closer look."

The trio trudged through the tall grass, noticing as they neared the mound that it was covered in a mass of vines.

"That's kudzu," Darius told them. "It grows crazy fast in the South. It kind of takes over trees and other plants so they can't get any sunlight."

"Is it poisonous?" Delta asked. She'd gotten into poison ivy before, and it made her itch something awful.

"Nah. In fact, some people make jelly from it."

"Like, jelly to eat?" Jax said. "Gross!"

The kids had gotten close enough to the Indian mound to notice a set of wooden stairs up one side, with a series of informational signs along the way. The first sign was positioned at the base of the steps.

"It says this is the Santee Indian Mound, and it was built over hundreds of years," Darius told them.

"Like Santy Claus!" Jax laughed.

Darius smiled. "More like the Santee tribe. They were the Native Americans that lived around here for hundreds of years before the American settlers took over. This says the pyramid grew higher each time a chief died. Then, when it got really tall, they built a temple on the top of it."

"So, it's a burial mound?" Delta gulped. All three kids looked at the hill before them. How many chiefs had been buried here over the centuries to make such an imposing mound?

The trio started up the steep steps, stopping here and there at landings to catch their breath and read additional signs.

"This one says that, during the Revolutionary War, the British Army destroyed the abandoned temple on top of the mound and replaced it with a fort called Fort Watson," Delta said.

Jax frowned. "I bet the ghosts of those chiefs didn't like that much!"

Delta couldn't help but think of poor Constance True, the one they called the Sea Witch, supposedly haunting the Hilton Head islanders for disrespecting her. Did the Native American chiefs do the same to those who had disrespected them? Tearing down a sacred temple, even if the ones who built it were long gone, seemed wrong—like vandalizing an old cemetery. *Exactly* like that, in fact.

"Super cool, guys! Come look at this!" Jax had raced to the top of the stairs and was standing on top of the burial mound.

"Where's the British fort?" Delta asked as she and Darius caught up with her brother. Other than the wooden platform they were standing on, the flat top of the mound was nothing but vegetation.

"The Americans knocked it down after they won a battle here," Jax said. "And guess who was leading that particular battle for the Americans?" He grinned broadly.

"Francis Marion?" Delta guessed.

"Ding! Ding! Ding! We have a winner!"

"That must have been tricky," Darius said. "I mean, look how high up we are. I know Marion was supposed to be sneaky in the swamps, but it would be hard to sneak up on anybody up here."

"Plus, there was a fort on top of this hill then, so it would have been even higher," Delta said. The kids looked out over the surrounding landscape. Below them, the open meadow stretched out in every direction. Beyond the meadow was dense forest and, to their right, just beyond the tree line, the kids could just see Lake Marion—water that would have been the much narrower Santee River during the time of Fort Watson. From this high vantage point, Delta, Jax, and Darius could see for a mile in every direction.

"How could a group of Patriots way down there outsmart the British way up here?" Delta asked.

"The Swamp Fox outfoxed them!" Jax said with a grin, pointing to the hill-top historical marker.

Darius examined the marker and smiled. "That's sure the truth! It says the Americans tried for weeks to defeat the British in the fort, but they could never get close to the hill."

"I imagine not," Delta said. "The fort kept the British troops safe. They would have seen the Americans coming and shot down at them."

"Until one of Marion's men came up with a genius idea!"

"Maybe it was Mr. Talbird," Jax suggested.

"No, somebody named Major Maham," Darius corrected. "Anyway, the Americans spent three days chopping down trees in the woods nearby."

"To build a big fire?" Delta asked.

Darius shook his head. "Nope, they spent three days chopping down trees until they had a whole slew of notched logs—like giant Lincoln Logs."

"We have some of those back in Chicago," Jax said.

Darius nodded. "Then, in the middle of the night, the Americans rolled their logs close to the mound and built a giant stacked tower out of them—tall enough to look right down inside Fort Watson!"

Delta was starting to get the picture. "So, the British soldiers woke up to Americans firing right down into their super secure hilltop fort?"

Darius grinned. "Exactly. They never saw them coming."

Jax laughed. "I can just picture the guys in that fort. One day, they're shouting down at the Patriots, 'Na na na, you can't get us!' And then the next day, they're toast!"

Delta looked out again over the lands below. General Marion had indeed outfoxed his opponents. He had taken what seemed to be an impossible problem and found a solution by literally looking at the situation in a new way. Could a new perspective solve their modern-day troubles, too?

13

Floating the Swamp

"The Lake Marion fish lived to see another day," Mac said as he drove the group back to their campsite. "We didn't land one keeper."

"No, but that's not what fishing is about," Pops said. "It's really just an excuse to enjoy the scenery and the quiet for a while. I'd say it was a successful morning in that sense—once you kids headed down the trail, that is." He winked at the kids sitting in the backseat of the SUV.

"It was really cool, Pops. Did you know there used to be a British fort on top of the mound you told us about? Francis Marion tricked the army up there by building a log tower even taller than the fort."

"Yeah," Jax added. "And the Patriots fired right down at them! It was an aerial attack!"

Pops chuckled. "I suppose it was."

Mac pulled into the gravel parking space at the campsite, and everyone piled out of the car.

"What's for lunch, Pops?" Jax asked. "I'm starving!"

"Fresh fish, of course."

Delta scowled. "But we didn't catch anything."

With a smile, Mac lifted the lid of the large cooler they'd brought from home. "Ta da!" he said, producing a package wrapped in white paper and sealed in a plastic bag. "Plan B! I stopped at Benny Hudson's Seafood Market right before we left home yesterday. This flounder has been on ice ever since."

"Wow, Dad." Darius grinned. "You must have had no faith in our fishing skills."

"Yeah," Jax added. "What if we'd actually caught something in the lake today? I mean, besides Delta's stick."

"Hardy har har," she said, rolling her eyes.

"No problem at all," Pops said. "We'd have just eaten more!"

Thirty minutes later, with the aroma of fried fish filling their campsite, the crew gobbled down the last of the flounder. Darius poked at the coals of the campfire with a sturdy stick he'd found nearby, and they all watched as tiny sparks flew up and then extinguished.

"I'm stuffed," Jax said, and everyone nodded in agreement.

"Looks like somebody is still hungry, though," Pops whispered, nodding toward a sweetgum tree edging the woods behind the tent. Peeking from behind the trunk was a bright orange fox.

"It probably smelled our lunch," Delta whispered, and her grandfather nodded.

The group sat silently for several minutes, watching as the animal observed them. Finally, the fox twitched its fluffy tail and, in a blink, turned and disappeared into the forest.

"It didn't seem afraid of us at all!" Delta said.

"It was just curious to see what we were doing," Mac said. "Once it sensed we were no threat, there was no need to be afraid."

"Hey, speaking of foxes," Pops said, "since you kiddos seem interested in the Swamp Fox, Mac and I came up with an idea. Instead of canoeing on the lake this afternoon, what would you think of kayaking in the Puddin' Swamp, just like old Francis Marion himself

70

used to do?"

"He used a kayak?"

"Well, no, Jackson. He likely had flat-bottom boats or marsh tackies, or just waded through. But the outfitter we're using has kayaks."

"Sounds great!" Darius said, and Delta and Jax agreed. "Let's head to the swamp!"

Delta eased the bright red kayak into the black waters of Puddin' Creek. Tiana, their professional guide for the swamp trip, had assigned each member of the group his or her own life jacket and vessel, with a double-ended paddle ideal for solo maneuvering. Delta was used to Pops's two-person kayak, which she and Jax often took out on the narrow canal behind their grandparents' house. It would be a treat to ride alone today, free to move at her own pace and in her own direction.

"Puddin' Swamp's a funny name," Jax noted as they climbed into their kayaks and began paddling in the wake of their guide.

"The story goes that there was a woman who lived near here on a rice plantation," Tiana said. "She used to help out the Swamp Fox and his men by feeding them, but she only served rice pudding. They started calling this spot Puddin' Swamp in honor of her."

"I'd rather have chocolate pudding," Jax said.

Tiana laughed. "Then you'd have to find somebody with a chocolate plantation. None of those around here, I'm afraid."

Tiana had prepared them for the bigger fears they could face ahead—hidden obstructions beneath the black water, pesky mosquitos, snakes, and alligators.

"Oh, yeah, we have gators on Hilton Head, too," Jax had told her. "And we have marshes, which are the same as swamps."

"Close, but not exactly the same," she had said. "Your marshes are salt water and are fed by tidal changes. I'll bet there are lots of grasses there."

"That's right," Delta said.

"Instead of grasses, swamps have trees, and don't change with a tide. Think of them more like freshwater-flooded forests. So not exactly the same as a marsh."

"But we do have alligators back home," Jax said.

Tiana smiled. "Well, just like back home, then, stay away from alligators. This is their home, and we're just visiting."

Delta quickly got into a tempo of dipping her paddle into the water, first the left side, then the right, then left again. Each time the tip disappeared beneath the surface, she would pull backward, propelling herself deeper into the swamp.

Even though it was early afternoon, their surroundings grew darker with every stroke of her paddle. They had entered the water at a landing not far from the highway, but now, as they traveled further from the bustle and noise of civilization, their passage grew narrow, and the tree cover was heavier. Gnarled water oak branches reached across the swamp, dripping with Spanish moss—a familiar reminder of home back on Hilton Head. On either side of the waterway, trees and foliage rose in an enveloping wall of forest. It was easy to imagine how that dense growth could camouflage animals—or militia men—hiding in its cover.

Darius paddled his kayak close to Delta's. "Just think—Mr. Talbird may have been in this very swamp with Francis Marion," he whispered. "Isn't it weird to think we were just reading about them this morning?"

"Especially since Maddy wrote about them, in 1781, just last night," Delta replied softly.

The group paddled in silence for several minutes, taking in the wild environment that enveloped them. Birds squawked invisibly as an autumn breeze whispered through the swaying leaves above.

Delta glanced back down at her paddle, hypnotized by its rhythmic movements.

"Why is the water so dark?" she asked. She was used to the murky green waters of the ocean and marshes of Hilton Head. Pops had explained how the murkiness there was the sign of a thriving community of tiny plankton as well as sand particles churned up from crashing waves on the seashore. She'd also seen muddy lakes back in Illinois, but this was different. Rather than resemble pea soup or creamy hot cocoa like those other waters, the liquid in the swamp gave the impression of clear black coffee.

"The answer is all around you," Tiana said with a smile. "Plants grow up from beneath the surface and leaves and other foliage drop into it from above. As all this vegetation decays, it leaves behind chemicals called 'tannins' that stain the water black, like a cup of tea. It also makes the water acidic, which leaves it low in nutrients."

"And since there aren't many nutrients in it, it's transparent?"

"That's right, Delta," Tiana said. "Clear, but dark."

The guide suddenly spun her kayak around so she was facing the rest of the group. Delta slowed her own vessel to a stop, wondering what was happening.

"We'll need to go single file up ahead," Tiana called so that everyone could hear her. "We're heading through an area known as Hell's Gate."

That sounds ominous, Delta thought.

"Keep to the left and make a sharp turn around that bend," Tiana added. "Don't worry if you get stuck; I'll get you out."

Tiana led the way through the narrow passage, hemmed in by two cypress trees as big around as Pops's backyard patio. Delta began to follow but was quickly stopped by an invisible barrier beneath the water.

"Something's not letting me pass," she called to Tiana.

"There are a lot of fallen logs just under the surface of the water. In fact, I bumped over one as I went through that same spot. Tell you what, do you know how to paddle backwards?"

Delta nodded. Her experience kayaking in Pops's canal was paying off. She dipped one end of her paddle into the water and focused on pushing the water forward instead of pulling it back. She used the same tactic on the other side and alternated strokes until she bumped into a kayak behind her.

"Hey!" Jax said.

"Sorry."

"There you go. That should be far enough," Tiana said. "Now, try again as fast as you can. When you hit the trunk, just keep on going. You should go right over top of it."

Delta was skeptical, but decided to trust Tiana, who made this trek all the time. "Full speed ahead!" she called, paddling forward with all her might. When she got to the underwater barricade, she powered on through, the front end of her kayak lifting momentarily and then dropping to the water with a splash as it crossed to the other side.

"I did it! It worked!" Delta lifted her paddle in the air, pumping it in celebration. She had squeezed between the trunks and triumphed over the sunken log, but the view on the other side stopped her cold.

14

Dealing with Danger

"What are all these things sticking up out of the water?" she asked. All around her, blocking her way, hundreds of woody projections rose from the swamp, some more than two feet tall. "Are they tree trunks?"

"Not exactly," Tiana replied. "Those are cypress knees. They develop from the roots of all these cypress trees growing around here."

"So, will new trees sprout from them or something?"

Tiana shook her head. "Nope. Some people say they provide extra air for the trees, and some think they secure the trees in the muddy swamp bottom, but no one knows for sure."

"Pops will know," Jax called from directly behind Delta. "He knows everything. Pops, what's the purpose of a cypress knee?"

From farther back in the swamp, Delta heard her grandfather's laugh.

"Sorry to disappoint you, Jackson, but this one is a mystery to me, too. If I ever hear that scientists have it figured out, I'll be sure to let you know."

Delta wove her kayak through the maze created by the protruding growths, glancing up to admire the giant cypresses that had created them. Tiana followed her gaze.

"You know, a lot of the trees in Puddin' Swamp were here five hundred years before the Revolutionary War. See that one over there, with that massive hollow trunk? A militia man and his gun could have hidden right there."

Delta imagined Mr. Talbird concealed within the damp lair, ready to fire at a Tory at any moment.

"And right here," Tiana continued, "looks like some critter had breakfast there this morning."

Delta looked at the spot where Tiana had pointed. At the base of a majestic cypress tree, its trunk shaped like a lady's hoop skirt, lay a cluster of tiny clamshells emptied of their meat.

"These trees were already ancient when Francis Marion called this place home," Tiana told them.

"He didn't actually *live* in the swamp, did he?" Jax asked, catching up with the guide.

"Sometimes, he did. Like the rest of his militia, he had a regular house when he wasn't fighting. But deep within these woods is a spot called Snow Island. It has enough solid ground that Marion and his men could camp there for weeks at a time. They would sneak out when there were British armies nearby, attack them, and then head back to Snow Island."

"And the British guys couldn't find them there?"

"Not a chance. Do you think *you* could find their campsite in this swamp?" Tiana asked with a grin.

The siblings glanced around at the dense forest surrounding them. Water spread out in every direction, providing countless routes through towering trees, draping vines, and cypress knees rising like stalagmites from the opaque surface of the swamp. Without Tiana to guide them, they could probably paddle around in here for days without finding their way out. It was amazing to think that Marion and his men could manage it so easily. No wonder the British soldiers couldn't catch them.

Delta was deep in thought when a loud splash near the shore startled her. Was that a gator that had just entered the water? She'd encountered gators on the island and wasn't eager to do so again.

Allowing room for the others to pass through the maze of Hell's Gate, she paddled just a bit farther on, leaving Tiana and Jax behind to coax the others through the constrictive passage. Making sure she could still hear their voices, she found herself in a wider body of water, still shrouded on all sides by foliage and thick with cypress knees.

She watched dappled sunlight through the trees sparkle on the ebony water, dancing with a cluster of water bugs on the mirror-like surface. Delta lifted her face and breathed in the crisp fall air. Aside from the natural sounds of birds, insects, and wind through the trees, this isolated spot was silent. It was hard to imagine that this peaceful place had been a combat zone during Maddy's lifetime.

The sudden flight of the water-bug clan caught Delta's attention. A dark shadow, barely distinguishable against the water's surface, was betrayed only by its movement. A long, undulating line, with a bright red-orange belly and head raised into the air.

"Snake!" Delta yelled and, in her panic, tipped her kayak completely over.

Splash!

Delta had capsized a kayak before in the Hilton Head salt marshes, but she'd merely gotten muddy from that mishap. This time, she was standing in waist-deep water, watching the snake continue its approach—unable to see anything that might be attacking her from below. There could be a gator on the prowl, blood-sucking leeches, or biting catfish. These were all distinct possibilities, but the swamp snake was definitely headed right toward her.

Her feet were beginning to sink in the mucky bottom of the

swamp, so she made the quick decision to swim. Although she couldn't make out any obviously solid ground within easy reach, Delta splashed desperately toward the water's edge, her life jacket rising uncomfortably around her chin. Meanwhile, the snake continued its pursuit.

"Ow!" Delta yelled, a stinging sensation burning her hand. She clambered atop a cluster of cypress knees, awkwardly balancing on the knobby tips. She closed her eyes and waited for the snake's venom to take effect.

Suddenly, Delta heard a smack behind her. She opened her eyes just in time to see a wriggling four-foot snake fly through the air above her as if in slow motion. It landed on the far bank with a slap, apparently disoriented by its recent flight. Without a sound, a pumpkin-colored fox appeared from behind a water oak, snatched the snake in its mouth, and vanished into the surrounding forest.

"Did you see that?" Jax yelled. "I picked it up with my paddle and tossed it into the woods. I saved your life!"

Tiana had reached Delta by this time and helped her flip her kayak and climb back in.

"I think it bit me!" Delta said, holding back tears. "Am I going to be okay?"

Tiana carefully inspected Delta's outstretched hand and then smiled. "You lucked out, my friend. You don't have a snake bite. It looks like you got scraped on a branch is all. It was probably under the water where you couldn't see it. I've got a first aid kit in my kayak that'll fix you right up."

Embarrassed and relieved, Delta allowed their guide to clean and treat her scratch, covering it with a waterproof bandage. By then, Darius, Mac, and Pops had all made it through Hell's Gate, and the group had reconvened. Everyone was thankful that Delta's snake encounter had turned out as well as it had.

"That's the second time today that a stick's gotten the best of you,

Delta-boo," Pops said with a wink.

"I could have really gotten a snake bite, Pops!"

"There definitely are some poisonous snakes in the swamp," Tiana said, "but that particular one was black with a bright orange belly, right?"

"Sort of reddish-orange," Delta said.

Tiana nodded. "That's a Carolina Swamp Snake. Fortunately, that breed isn't venomous and isn't harmful to humans at all. If you were a fish or a tadpole, though, you'd need to watch out. Those are a Swamp Snake's favorite snacks."

"We've had a bit of excitement here, but you're all doing great!" Tiana added. "Why don't we rest for a few minutes and rehydrate?"

Everyone opened their water bottles and guzzled. They had already paddled a couple of miles and could use a break. Now that her bottom half was wet from her time in the water, Delta felt the October chill and looked for the nearest spot of sunlight to dry off. Mac and Pops pulled their kayaks close to their guide's to inquire more about local swamp plants, giving the kids time to chat privately.

"Are you okay?" Darius asked.

"I'll be fine. Let's just forget it."

"Don't forget that I saved your life!" Jax said.

"Thank you for that, but please, let's just forget it."

To appease his friend, Darius changed the subject. "It's pretty amazing how the Swamp Fox could slip in and out of places to attack his enemies. Sounds like he never got caught doing it, either. I wish we could figure out how our own Marsh Fox managed to mess up the cemetery."

"Why do you call him that, Darius?" Delta asked. "Marion attacked by water, but the cemetery is inland, isn't it?"

"I just meant whoever it is was as *sneaky* as a fox. He—or she— slipped in and out without anyone seeing them."

"We know who it was!" Jax said. "It was definitely a *he* because it was Enzo! He probably just slithered like a snake into that cemetery on Sunday night and then slithered back out after he'd done all the damage. He ought to be the one getting in trouble, and I can't wait until he does!"

"Wait just a minute now," Mac said, alerted by Jax's raised voice. "Don't you kids go blaming Enzo for the vandalism. That's how rumors get started."

"But we really think he might have done it, Dad!" Darius said. "He was mad that we didn't invite him to go with us that night. Plus, he's spreading rumors all over school about us!"

"So, you want to get revenge by spreading one about him?" Mac asked.

"It's not a rumor if it's true," Jax said.

"That's just the problem, though," Mac said. "It isn't true that Enzo went to the cemetery last Sunday."

"How can you know that, Dad?"

"I know it for a fact because Keisha wanted to have a sleepover with Enzo's sister Maria last Sunday. It didn't happen because Maria *and her brother* were in Savannah all day Sunday with their dad. They didn't come home until Monday morning, when Keisha went to Maria's house for a playdate. Remember? You were all at our house when she got back home."

"When she gave us the acorns," Darius said.

Delta, Jax, and Darius sat quietly for a moment. Finally, Delta spoke.

"I'm sorry, Mac. I guess we jumped to conclusions. We just want so badly to find out who really did the damage so that we don't get the blame."

Mac nodded. "I get it. But it doesn't help matters to go blaming the wrong person. If you did that, then Enzo would be hurting like you are—blamed for something he didn't do. You don't want to be the cause of that, do you?"

"No, sir," Darius said, and Delta shook her head.

"I still can't stand Enzo," Jax whispered as Mac paddled his kayak out of earshot. "He lied about us to everyone."

"Yeah, but Mac's right," Delta said. "Lying about him doesn't fix anything."

Jax sighed. "I thought revenge was supposed to be sweet."

"We're not after revenge, Jax," Darius reminded him. "But now we're back to square one. If Enzo isn't our Marsh Fox, then who is?"

15

Playing with Time

Thankfully, the group's return to the boat landing passed uneventfully, aside from Mac paddling directly into an enormous spiderweb that spanned the channel. Once it was confirmed that no spiders were involved, everyone had a good chuckle over the encounter, even Mac himself. Rather than endure Hell's Gate for a second time, Tiana had led them back via an alternate route.

"Are you sure this is different?" Darius asked. "It looks just like the way we came."

Tiana smiled. "I'm sure. You can see, though, how someone could easily get lost in here. To the untrained eye, every tree and cypress knee look pretty much the same."

"How could the Swamp Fox find his way around?" Delta asked. "I mean, if everything is identical."

"That's just it," Tiana replied. "It isn't identical at all if you know where to look. For example, remember that big hollow tree we passed earlier, the one I said could hide a man?" The kids nodded. "Marion and his men would have used that as a landmark. And notice how that group of cypress knees are lined up in a stairstep pattern?"

Delta followed the guide's gaze to a series of knobs protruding from the water. Measured from the surface, the one on the left was only a few inches high, with the one next to it twice that height. The pattern continued through six adjacent cypress knees, making the final product appear to be a set of stairs.

"Marion's militia might have given that formation a name like 'Satan's Steps' or something, to help them remember it. They'd have had a whole bunch of those subtle landmarks memorized to help them find their hideout."

"Or to help them find their way out of the swamp," Delta added.

"Exactly," Tiana agreed as they paddled around a bend and caught sight of the wooden landing. "Getting out is even more important than getting in."

The first thing Delta did when the SUV arrived at their campsite was head down the path to the campground's bathhouse for a hot shower. After several hours in cold, wet blue jeans, it felt great to put on a warm pair of leggings and her favorite University of South Carolina sweatshirt.

She strolled back up the gravel path just as the sun was dipping behind the shedding trees, the smell of smoke in the air. As she approached the campsite, she could see a fire already blazing within the metal ring.

"Ooh! That's going to feel great!" she said, raising her hands to the warmth emanating from the dancing flames. Darius was kneeling nearby, placing foil packets in the coals at the edge of the fire.

"Hope you don't mind that we went ahead and started dinner," he said.

"I don't mind at all," Delta said. "What are we having?"

"Hobos. They're a camping classic, you know."

"Yeah," Jax chimed in. "We had them at Boy Scout camp. You just put in a hamburger patty, some chopped onions, carrots, and potatoes, and then season it all with salt and pepper."

"I like a little hot sauce on mine," Mac said. "Mm, mm, good!"

About twenty minutes later, the crew was seated in folding chairs around the campfire, eagerly digging into their meals. Swamp exploration had apparently made them all quite hungry.

"What's for dessert?" Jax asked before he'd even finished his meal.

"Banana boats for everyone!" Pops announced.

Delta, Jax, Darius, and the adults each sliced open an unpeeled banana lengthwise. Pulling the slit open slightly, they carefully stuffed it full of mini-marshmallows and chocolate chips. After wrapping each banana in aluminum foil, they placed them all near the fire's coals, just as they'd done with the hobos.

"These don't take as long," Darius explained. "Nothing's really cooking. We just need to melt the chocolate and marshmallows." Within five minutes, they were scooping the gooey treat from inside the banana peels.

"*Omigosh*, this is so good!" Delta scraped every last bit of sweetness out of her peel before wrapping the remains in the foil and placing it in a trash bag in the back of the SUV. They had done the same with their hobo packets, so cleanup was a breeze. The campground had provided each site with its own trashcan, but Mac had suggested they not use it.

"I'd rather not be woken up in the middle of the night by some rowdy raccoons digging in our trash," he'd said. "It'll be safer in the car."

"Who'll join me in singing some campfire songs?" Pops asked after everyone had finished eating. When no one jumped at that idea, he suggested a different diversion. "How about a game of Time Machine?"

Based on a classic book by H.G. Wells about time travel, Pops and

SUSAN DIAMOND RILEY

his grandkids had invented the game years ago. It had been a favorite of Delta's and Jax's for as long as they could remember. Given their shared last name, Pops had always said the author could be an ancestor of theirs. Delta didn't know for sure, but the game was fun either way.

"It's great, Darius!" she told her friend. "You just pretend that you've visited some place and time in history."

"Or the future," Jax added.

"True, or the future. And you share something you saw or did there. Each person can take a turn adding to the story until we run out of ideas."

"Sure, I'm in," Darius said.

Mac agreed. "Count me in, too."

"Okay, I've got a good one," Delta said. "Can I start?"

Pops and Jax glanced at each other and smiled. Then, in unison, they asked, "Been anytime interesting lately?"

Mac and Darius both raised their eyebrows in surprise.

"Oh, we forgot to tell you, that's how we start the game," Delta explained, before turning to her grandfather and brother. "Let's start over."

Not quite in unison, Pops, Jax, Darius, and Mac asked Delta, "Been anytime interesting lately?" This time she replied.

"Funny you should ask. I spent a lovely afternoon yesterday in ancient Egypt. The weather was sunny and dry, and I read the most interesting book while I was there. Actually, it was more of a carving on the wall of the temple to the sun god, Ra. It was written in hieroglyphics and told the story of a greedy old pharaoh who filled his tomb with gold for the afterlife rather than leave it to his family."

Darius laughed. "You can read hieroglyphics but not cursive?"

Delta smiled. "It's just a game." She pointed to her brother. "Your turn."

"After my time in the temple, I wandered across the sand and saw

85

a boat coming up the Nile River. The pharaoh was lying on a bench, and servants were feeding him grapes and fanning him with ginormous palm branches."

"The same pharaoh that put all his gold in the tomb?" Darius asked.

"Shh," Delta whispered. "Wait your turn."

"No, it was a different pharaoh," Jax clarified. "He was wearing a white robe thingy and a fancy golden collar necklace with gobs of jewels in it. And his hair was chopped off straight across at his shoulders, and he had these goofy straight-across bangs, too." Jax placed his hand flat against his forehead to demonstrate. "Oh, and I almost forgot! While I was watching, a crocodile ate a hippopotamus in the river!"

"Actually, I've heard that hippopotamuses . . ." Darius began.

"It's hippopotami," Jax corrected.

"No, that's a common mistake. It really is hippopotamuses," Darius continued. "Anyway, I read that they are some of the most vicious animals in Africa. They wouldn't be an easy mark for a crocodile."

Jax frowned. "Well, since you know so much, why don't you take a turn then?"

Darius cleared his throat. "Okay, let's see. Um, yeah. So, I saw this pharaoh on a boat, and then I thought a crocodile was going to eat a hippo, but instead, the hippo scared the *bejeezus* out of the croc, and it swam away. But then . . ." Darius paused, out of ideas.

"Just say something you know about ancient Egypt," Delta suggested.

Darius nodded. "Okay, so then I died, and some people removed all of my vital organs, pulled my brain out through my nose, and turned me into a mummy."

"That's so gross!" Delta squealed.

Jax grinned. "Awesome!"

"Way to end the story, D," Mac laughed. "You killed off the main character."

"Let me start a new one," Pops said. He held his index fingers up as if he were conducting an orchestra. When he pointed them at the others, they all recited in unison.

"Been anytime interesting lately?"

"You'll never believe it," Pops said seriously. "Just this morning, I was wandering through the woods right here in the upcountry of South Carolina, hiking along near the Santee River, and who should jump out in front of me but Colonel Francis Marion! Of course, it was right during the Revolutionary War, so what did I expect?"

"He had a musket in his hand," Pops continued, "and before I knew it, he was holding a bayonet to my chest."

"'Friend or foe?' he says."

"'Friend, of course,' I replied. I didn't tell him that I wasn't taking sides. I sure didn't want to get caught up in a battle with the British! But pretty soon, I no longer had a choice . . .'"

Pops pointed across the campfire at his friend. "You take it, Mac."

Mac thought for a few seconds before continuing the tale. "We saw their red coats before they saw us. It was a band of about a dozen British soldiers and their Tory allies."

"Wait," Jax said. "What's the difference between 'British' and 'Tory'?"

"They were fighting for the same side against the Patriots," Pops explained, "but British soldiers were actually from England. Tories were American colonists who were still loyal to the King."

"Oh, yeah," Jax replied. "Sorry, Mac. Go ahead."

Mac began again. "'Follow me, friend,' the Swamp Fox said to me, so I raced behind him into the swamp. We hopped from cypress knee to fallen log, and occasionally waded through gator-infested waters, until we arrived at Snow Island—the hideout of Marion and his men. Several members of his militia were lazing on the little hummock of land until they saw their leader arrive. They jumped up immediately when Marion told them, 'We've got a battle to win, boys.'"

Mac paused, and everyone leaned forward in anticipation. What was going to happen next? But then, he smiled and pointed to his son.

"You're up, D."

"Okay, so I'm one of Marion's men, and I was excited for a battle but also kind of scared."

"You're not supposed to switch characters midway through, Darius," Delta said, but Pops waved his hand.

"It's fine. No hard and fast rules to this game. We're just having fun."

Darius began again. "So, I fight in Francis Marion's militia, but I'm really a plantation owner from Hilton Head. I wanted to help the Patriots win independence for our country, but it made me sad to leave my wife behind because she was expecting a baby."

Suddenly Delta realized what Darius was doing. He was being Mr. Talbird.

"Anyway, we headed to Eutaw Springs to face our enemies. There was smoke everywhere from muskets firing, and the guy next to me got stabbed with a bayonet. I didn't get hurt, but the Tories caught me and took me to Charleston, where they put me on a prison ship in the middle of the harbor." Darius pointed at Jax to continue.

"Hello, I'm that guy's neighbor's daughter, back on Hilton Head."

Pops laughed. "We've gone a little off the rails here . . ."

Jax cleared his throat loudly and continued. "I'm eleven years old, and my dad is probably a plantation owner on Hilton Head, too. He's in the local militia and I worry about him having to fight in this war. I wish it would end soon before anybody else gets captured or killed."

Jax stopped talking, but he didn't point to anyone else. Suddenly, Delta, whose turn it should have been next, realized she didn't feel like playing this game anymore. Since they'd read those journal entries from Maddy, Jax's story was just too real.

"I'm getting kind of tired," she said. "Can we stop for the night?"

Across the circle, through the glow of the dancing flames, Delta could see Darius nod his head in agreement.

"Why don't you kiddos go brush your teeth and get ready to hit the sack?" Pops asked. "Between Delta getting attacked by a snake, Jax having to save her life, and Darius being mummified in ancient Egypt, it's been a mighty big day. Who knows what could happen tomorrow?"

16

Considering the Suspects

The trio grabbed their flashlights, toothbrushes, and toothpaste from the tent and headed down the gravel path toward the bathhouse.

"Man, I was hoping he'd forget again tonight," Jax said, sticking his toothbrush in the pocket of his sweatshirt. "Oh, hey! Did I show you guys what I found?" He pulled his hand from his pocket and held out his open palm.

Delta shone her flashlight on her brother's hand and gasped. There sat a poof of carrot-colored fur the size of a baseball. "Where'd you get that?" she asked.

"It was stuck to the bark of that sweetgum tree behind the tent. Remember, where that fox was watching us this morning."

"I'd forgotten all about that!" she said.

"Me, too." Darius's brow furrowed. "Delta, didn't you say a fox ended up eating that snake that was after you in the swamp?"

"Well, I don't know if it ate the thing or not, but it picked the snake up in its mouth and ran away with it."

"My point is, isn't it strange that we've seen foxes twice in one day, on the exact day we're learning about the Swamp Fox?"

"Maybe it was the same fox," Jax said, "just in two different places."

Delta shook her head. "No, the one in the swamp was definitely bigger than the one at the campsite."

"Either way," Darius said, "it's a weird coincidence."

The trio stood quietly on the gravel path, staring at the tuft of fur. Delta gently touched it with her index finger.

"It's so soft. The poor little thing must have gotten its tail stuck on the rough tree trunk."

Darius laughed. "It's just fur. It's not like the whole tail came off!"

"Do you suppose either of those foxes was the Sea Witch?" Jax asked. "Remember, Ivy said Constance True sometimes appeared as a fox after she died."

"Some of the islanders *thought* she appeared as a fox," Darius said. "That doesn't mean she actually did."

"I think foxes just reminded them of Constance True because she had red hair," Delta said. "Maybe the people were just feeling guilty about what they'd done to her and so they were easily spooked."

Jax shrugged. "They said the Sea Witch hung out around water. With the lake and the swamp, there's lots of water around here. I think one of those foxes could've been her." He clearly wanted the tale to be true.

"So, you're saying the Sea Witch was in the swamp today, wanting me to capsize the kayak? You think she's still mad that we were telling stories about her in the cemetery?" Delta asked.

"That's one possibility," Jax said. "Or maybe she was there, but she wasn't trying to be bad. After all, she did take the snake away."

Darius patted Jax on the shoulder. "You're trying awfully hard to make these pieces fit, buddy, but I'm pretty sure they were just plain old foxes we saw today. Cool piece of fur, though."

Delta and Darius continued toward the bathhouse, with Jax

trailing behind them. He studied the orange ball of fluff in his hand. Sea Witch or not, he had plans for his discovery.

Suddenly, Darius spun on his heels to face Jax. "You mentioned the cemetery, though. That reminds me of something we haven't had a chance to discuss yet. Enzo's alibi."

Once again, the three huddled on the path. At this rate, they were never going to brush their teeth.

"Your dad seemed really sure that Enzo couldn't have been there Sunday night," Delta said.

Darius nodded. "I know. But if he didn't frame us, who did?"

"Maybe they weren't framing us specifically," Delta said. "I mean, lots of people have been hurt by this—even our families. You said business is really slow at your parents' restaurant, and Pops is in trouble with the city council."

"That's it!" Jax said. "I knew there was something suspicious about that lady."

"Who?"

"That city council lady, the one at the Fall Festival. She acted nice to everybody at first, but then she got all huffy when she found out that Micah and Ivy had been telling their Ghostly Tales at the cemetery. And she reamed Pops out good and said the museum shouldn't be allowed to have events at historical sites."

"That was before any real damage had even been done," Delta added, "but then she made an official complaint about the museum to the city council after the vandalism."

"Exactly!" her brother said. "There's your motive right there. She wanted an excuse to file a complaint."

"I don't know, y'all." Darius looked skeptical. "She didn't like people being at the cemetery at night because she thought something might get messed up there."

"Right!"

"But then why would she herself go mess something up? That is exactly what she did *not* want to happen. Plus, she's this professional woman and she's, like, my mom's age. I can't see her sneaking around in the dark with a can of spray paint. It just doesn't make sense."

"I guess," Delta said. "And anyway, whoever did it painted Micah's school symbol and initials on the wall of the mausoleum. I think they were trying to get *him* in trouble, not Pops."

"But who would want to hurt Micah? He's a really great guy, even to us little kids."

"Speak for yourself, Jax," Darius said. "Delta and I aren't that little."

"Didn't that guy Waldo make the original Island Neighbor post that alerted everybody to what had happened?" Delta asked.

"Well, the newspaper did that," Darius corrected, "but the social media post gave all kinds of obvious hints that Micah was involved."

"And Waldo was a real jerk to Ivy at the Fall Festival, all jealous because she got to be the team kicker instead of him."

"That's right, Jax," Darius said. "Remember how Micah got so mad and told him off?"

It was all coming back to Delta now. "And he was standing right across the room by the face painting table while we were planning our storytelling trip for Sunday night. He knew exactly where we were going and when."

"It all makes perfect sense," Darius said as the trio made one final attempt to reach the bathhouse and brush their teeth before bedtime. "So, how'd he get away with it?"

17

Heading Back Home

Delta awoke slowly the next morning. With her eyes still closed, she lay curled peacefully on her side in the warm flannel-lined sleeping bag. She had been dreaming of a pathway in a dense autumn forest. Brightly colored leaves had been falling around her like orange, red, and yellow confetti. Suddenly, a smiling fox had appeared in front of her, wearing a snake around its neck like a feather boa.

"Hello, my friend," the fox had said. "Do be careful of the Tories. They like to sneak up the creek when no one is looking, and then they're gone before you know it."

How strange? Delta thought as she lay there half awake. *I thought it was the Swamp Fox who did the sneaking—not the Tories.* She yawned loudly but was nearly drawn back to sleep by a soothing *tap-tap-tap* on the roof of the tent. That is, until her brother kicked her in the stomach.

"Oof! Geez, Jax! What's your problem?" A crack of thunder reverberated through the surrounding trees.

"Keep snoozing if you want," he said. "We'll just take the tent down and fold it up with you in it. How's that sound?"

Delta sat up and looked around her. Sure enough, everything—and everyone—in the tent, other than her, her sleeping bag, and her sneakers, were gone.

"It's pouring out, so we're breaking camp early," Jax explained. "Pops already put our gear in the car. Well, except for your sleeping bag." He tossed her a ball of plastic sheeting that turned out to be a rain poncho.

"Why didn't somebody wake me up?"

"We tried. You were snoring so loud, no one could stand to go near you."

"I was not!" Delta yelled as Jax headed back into the downpour.

Quickly rolling up her sleeping bag, Delta slipped into her shoes, still damp from yesterday's swamp swim, and pulled the poncho over her head. She emerged from the tent to find the back of the RV nearly filled with camping gear. As Mac, Pops, Darius, and Jax worked together to dismantle the tent, she stuffed her sleeping bag into a gap among the gear. Since there didn't appear to be a task for her at the moment, she climbed into the back seat of the car and sheltered from the storm.

Ten minutes later, the wet tent zipped into its carrying bag and secured tightly to the roof of the SUV, the soppy gang was headed back to Hilton Head. Instead of their planned breakfast of bacon and eggs cooked over a campfire, the group munched on homemade apple streusel coffee cake that Darius's mom had sent along as a treat.

"We'll need to set the tent back up as soon as we get home," Mac said.

"We're camping again tonight?" Delta asked.

"No, you always want to air out the tent after a campout," Darius explained.

Jax nodded. "You'd know that if you'd been to Boy Scout camp."

Delta stifled a yawn and rolled her eyes. "Yeah, well, I'm not a Boy

Scout, am I?"

"You could be," her brother said. "Girls can join too, now, you know."

"In any case," Mac said, "it's especially important to set the tent up today because we need to let it dry out before we store it. Otherwise, it'll mildew."

"What if it's raining back home, too, Dad? We were heading to Daufuskie this afternoon to see Bubba."

"Not a problem, Darius," Pops said. "The weather's all clear back in the Lowcountry. It should be a great day for Daufuskie."

Delta and the boys had napped during much of the ride home from Lake Marion, soothed by the swipe of the windshield wipers and the smooth jazz music Pops and Mac were playing on the car stereo. True to Pops's forecast, when they awoke back on Hilton Head, it was to sunny blue skies.

"Tell me all about your campout!" Tootsie called from the front steps as the Wells family exited Mac's SUV. Delta could tell her grandmother had been painting—her new fascination in retirement. Tootsie was wearing loose denim overalls with one of Pops's old white dress shirts over it like an unbuttoned lab coat. Bright splotches of turquoise, magenta, and lime green decorated her clothes—as well as her left cheek—as if she had been coloring with neon highlighter pens. Her spiky silver hair and sparkly red eyeglasses accented her vibrant outfit as she met the crew in the driveway.

"Did you have fun?" she asked, hugging Delta, Jax, and Pops in turn.

"It was a blast, Tootsie! Delta thought she'd been bitten by a snake, but it turned out to be just a scratch from a stick!"

Delta rolled her eyes. "Thanks for sharing that, Jax."

"I'll meet y'all at the ferry at one o'clock," Darius called as he and his dad backed out of the driveway.

Tootsie frowned. "The ferry? Where are ya'll going that you need to take a ferry?"

"Darius is taking us to Daufuskie Island," Delta explained. "He has a pet goat over there. Pops said it was okay."

"We can go, can't we, Tootsie?" Jax asked.

"Sure, you can, if that's what y'all had planned," Tootsie said. "But I'm giving a class at the museum later this afternoon and I thought you might enjoy it. I'll be talking about how paper has changed over the centuries and showing how to make your own paper from recycled materials."

Jax scowled. Delta figured the lesson sounded a bit educational for her brother's taste.

"What time is your class? Maybe we could catch the end of it?" Delta asked, hating to disappoint her grandmother. "It's just that we've already kind of promised Darius we would go with him to Daufuskie."

"Not a problem," Tootsie said with a smile and a wave of her hand. "I'll see you at the museum afterward."

The wall phone was ringing as the family walked through the front door. The harsh jangle of that old-timey contraption always startled Delta. She preferred the tweets, whistles, and songs most often heard on cell phones. Pops took the call while Delta and Jax carried their camping gear into the house.

"Put all the clothes directly into the laundry room," Tootsie told them. "Even the ones you didn't wear are going to smell like smoke from being stuffed in those bags with the dirty ones."

Pops was off the phone by the time the kids headed toward the kitchen for lunch. They could hear their grandparents' hushed voices from the hallway.

"They're voting on Monday morning," Pops was saying, "and apparently, it's not looking good for us."

"That is so unfair!" Tootsie said. "One incident and they're going to ban you from using any historic sites? It's the community that will lose out on that decision. The museum has hosted so many wonderful events at those places, and they've brought attention to the island's rich history!"

"You're preaching to the choir, hon," Pops said with a sigh.

The conversation ended abruptly when Delta and Jax appeared in the kitchen. They helped their grandparents make sandwiches, and then sat together, sharing their meal. Jax regaled Tootsie with tales of their camping adventures, but Delta couldn't stop thinking about what she'd overheard. It must have been someone from the city council on the phone talking to Pops, and it sounded like the museum was, in fact, going to be punished for the damage at the Zion Cemetery.

Delta felt her heart pound and heat rise to her face as she considered all the damage that had been done by last week's vandalism. Sure, tombstones had been knocked down and the mausoleum had been graffitied, which was bad enough. But that damage was just the tip of the iceberg—people had been hurt! Okay, not physically, but in ways that still counted. Pops's reputation as the head of the museum was at stake, Mac and Miss Ruby were losing business at their restaurant, and Micah might not even get to go to college! Not to mention that Delta, Jax, and Darius would likely be social misfits at school from now on (not that they were the coolest, most popular kids to begin with, but still). And when Mom and Dad finally got an internet connection and found out the trouble the kids were in . . . Delta couldn't even bring herself to go there.

All for something the kids didn't even do.

I know exactly how you feel, Constance True! Delta thought. *Sea Witch or not, I don't blame you for wanting revenge. And when we find out who did this to us, I want them to pay!*

18

Boating to Daufuskie

On their way to the museum, Pops and Tootsie dropped their grandkids at the ferry terminal on Broad Creek. Darius and Micah were already waiting on the wharf.

"Y'all almost missed the boat!" Darius said. "It leaves in just a few minutes."

They all hurried down the narrow dock that extended far out over the marsh grasses into the deeper waters of the channel. Micah led the way across the gangplank and onto the boat that would take them to Daufuskie Island. They passed through a small outdoor deck stacked with suitcases and pet carriers, and then entered the interior cabin lined with cushioned seats. About a dozen other passengers were already aboard.

"Are all these people going to see your goat?" Jax asked as the group found an empty row of seats in the front of the ferry.

"Yeah, right." Darius smiled.

"I was just kidding," Jax said.

"I know," Darius reassured him. "Some of them might be going to Daufuskie for vacation, like to rent a condo or something, or maybe they have a vacation home there. I imagine some of them live there all the time and are just coming home from work."

"What do you mean?" Delta asked.

"Well, there aren't a lot of places to work on Daufuskie, so a lot of people who live there work on Hilton Head or on the mainland. They commute back and forth on the ferry."

"Cool!" Jax said. "Like some people in Chicago commute on the train."

"And the kids who live there commute to and from school on the ferry," Micah said. "They catch a school bus at the ferry terminal on Hilton Head, and it takes them the rest of the way to school."

Jax grinned. "That would be so much fun!"

The kids watched through a wall of windows as the ferry pulled away from the dock, slowly at first, and then picked up speed as it entered the center of the wide waterway.

"I always thought it was strange that they call this a creek," Delta said. "It's wider than most rivers I've seen!" Sure enough, the homes lining either side appeared like tiny Monopoly buildings far in the distance.

"Well, it is called *Broad* Creek," Jax pointed out.

Delta shrugged. "Still, it's not creek-sized."

"Up at the north end it is," Micah said. "We're heading down toward Calibogue Sound on the south end of the island right now, but at the other end, Broad Creek narrows until it's just a trickle."

"Huh." Delta craned her neck to see the view behind them. She guessed she knew from looking at maps of Hilton Head that Broad Creek ended at some point. It went right up the middle of the tennis-shoe-shaped island, from south to north and toe to tongue, right where the shoes laces would be. Then, rather than completely bisect the island, it stopped somewhere before reaching Port Royal Sound on the northern coast. She'd never thought about it getting narrower at that end.

Music interrupted Delta's thoughts, and she realized that Micah had answered his cell phone. The constant hum of the ferry's engine drowned out neighboring conversations, and Micah had to shout to be heard over the noise.

"Yes, sir. I understand, but you do realize that no charges have been brought? I mean, I haven't officially been accused of anything. I would never do something like that. You've got to believe me!"

As Micah's voice rose in volume, Delta glanced around the cabin to see that other passengers were watching. As if suddenly realizing the attention he was drawing, Micah turned toward the window and lowered his voice a bit.

"Yes, sir. It's just that I was kind of counting on this scholarship." Micah listened as his caller spoke, and then sighed heavily. "Yes, sir. Please keep me posted." He stuffed the phone in the pocket of his football jacket and slumped in his seat.

"Was that somebody from the veterans group?" Darius asked his cousin.

Micah nodded. "They're meeting Tuesday night to decide on my scholarship. It doesn't look good, cuz." Micah was a tough-looking guy, but right then, it looked like he might cry. Delta felt like she might join him.

"Maybe we can find the real vandal before their meeting on Tuesday," Darius suggested.

"I don't know how, D," Micah said. "All evidence points to us, and I swear I don't think the sheriff is even looking anywhere else. I've asked around to see if any of the kids at school have heard anything, but it's just all about us—no other suspects."

"But they can't actually have enough evidence to prove we did it—because we didn't!" Darius said.

Micah shook his head. "As far as the veterans go, it doesn't even matter if I'm officially charged with anything. Just being accused is enough to 'tarnish the honor.' Those are the words the guy on the phone just used."

Darius flinched. "Ouch."

"Yeah, I don't want to talk about it anymore," Micah said, turning his back toward his cousin and staring out the window.

After a few moments of awkward silence, Darius suggested to Delta and Jax that the three of them head to the outside deck to see the view. They found a spot among the luggage and watched the distant shoreline flash past on either side. Fishing boats dotted Broad Creek as the ferry glided beneath the towering arch of the Cross Island Bridge— not the bridge to the mainland, but rather a connection between the two halves of the island bisected by the creek.

Once on the other side of the bridge, the ferry entered the larger Calibogue Sound, with views of the Atlantic Ocean in the distance. Small islets appeared here and there in the sound, some with individual houses built on them. Delta spied Hilton Head's red and white striped Harbour Town Lighthouse on the shore, with the green, less-developed Daufuskie Island looming across the dark water. The three kids watched as the ferry broke through the bobbing waves, cool mist splashing their faces.

"Hey, Jax," Darius said, using his jacket sleeve to wipe the salt spray from his glasses. "Since the rain caused all that craziness this morning, I never got to ask you. Was there a new journal entry today?"

Delta had completely forgotten about the journal. Come to think of it, she hadn't even had a chance to talk to Jax or Darius privately all day until now. "Yeah, was there another message from Maddy?"

Jax grinned and reached into his backpack. Pulling out the old diary, he handed it to Darius.

"Yes!" Darius said, turning to a brand-new entry and beginning to read aloud.

October 20, 1781

Dear GA,

Jamie has gone too far this time! There was a piece of orange fox fur in my box when I opened it! When I accused him of placing the Sea Witch's curse on me, he denied everything and cried to Mother. "Mercy Abigail Davant!" she said. "Be kind to your brother and behave like the loving older sister I know you to be." As if I were at fault! In any case, I do not know how to dispose of the wretched thing without transferring the curse to someone or something else. Yet, if I keep it, some horrible evil is sure to come upon my family from the waters around our island! Oh, Guardian Angel, what should I do?

"Fox fur?" Delta said, her brow furrowed. "Jax, did you . . ."

"I thought she'd think it was cool. How could I know she'd assume it was a curse?"

"Back then, the islanders saw foxes as a visitation from the Sea Witch," Darius reminded them. "Sounds like you kind of scared her to death."

Jax frowned. "I sure didn't mean to do that. I just wanted to give her another present for her box. I was trying to be nice."

"Well, at least we know who she really is now," Delta said. "'MAD' stands for 'Mercy Abigail Davant.' Ooh! I have an idea!" She pulled out her cell phone and tapped in Mercy's full name. A few seconds later, her smile fell.

"There's nothing on her here. It's as if she never existed."

"Well, she is just eleven," Jax said. "Most kids that age haven't done much newsworthy stuff yet."

"Yeah," Delta agreed, "but she didn't stay eleven forever. She would have eventually grown up and hopefully accomplished something."

"I hope so," Darius said. "But history tends to record more about the accomplishments of men than of women, especially from that era. I hate to say it, Delta, but it's pretty much true."

She hated to hear it, too, but knew her friend was right. Women in the past had undoubtedly contributed to society in countless ways, but just in recent years were those feats being more publicly recognized. Only select women had been remembered as a part of American history, and Mercy Abigail Davant was apparently not one of them. Delta sighed.

"Anyway, what else does Mercy write?"

> Papa and Colonel Marion have been having heated discussions with the local militia about the recent burnings of the Skull Creek plantations. The Tories claim the attack was retribution for one of their soldiers who was killed by a Hilton Head Patriot. Now Papa's militia has vowed revenge on the Daufuskie men. In fact, I overheard Papa tell Colonel Marion that he and the others are meeting tomorrow evening at the Muster House to carry out their retaliation. Oh, when will all the killing end? I cannot wait for this war to be over.
>
> Your ever faithful, MAD

"It's kind of funny, really," Darius said when he had finished reading and handed the journal back to Jax. "Not funny *haha*, but *strange* funny."

"How so?" Delta asked.

"Well, as far as Mercy and everybody on Hilton Head was

concerned back then, Daufuskie was an enemy island."

"I guess you're right," Delta said.

"And yet, here we are." Darius nodded to his left and the siblings followed his gaze.

"Welcome to Daufuskie Island," the sign looming over the ferry terminal stated. The boat pulled toward the dock as passengers gathered their belongings and prepared to disembark.

Jax squinted into the afternoon sun and then turned to Delta and Darius.

"You don't suppose we have any enemies here, do you?"

19

Visiting the Farm

Micah seemed slightly cheered by the sight of his friend Jon waiting for them at the ferry dock on Daufuskie.

"Hey, man! You made it!" Jon and Micah bumped fists. "How was the ride over?"

"It was great!" Jax said. "You're so lucky! Micah said you get to do that every day for school."

"Sort of," Jon said. "I don't usually take the ferry. I like to drive myself over."

"Drive?" Delta said. "But I thought there weren't any bridges to this island."

"That's right." Jon nodded. "By 'drive,' I meant drive one of my dad's boats over. Most everybody over here has at least one. That way, I don't have to stick to the ferry schedule."

"But you still have to stick to the school bus schedule," Jax said.

Jon and Micah looked at each other and laughed. "Seniors don't ride the bus if we can help it," Jon said. "I meet up with some friends at the marina on Hilton Head, and they drive me the rest of the way to school in their car."

The group headed down the dock and onto a gravel parking lot filled not with cars or trucks, but with dozens of golf carts.

"So, nobody here drives regular cars?" Delta asked.

"Think about it," Jax said. "How would they get them here? On the ferry?"

"Well, actually there are a few trucks here," Jon said. "They were brought here by barge and are mainly used by businesses. You know, for hauling building supplies and ship fuel. That sort of thing. That's all brought here by barges, too."

"For just getting around, people here use golf carts, though," Micah said. "Like Jon's." He motioned toward a vehicle that reminded Delta of the tram she and Jax had ridden on in the Disney World parking lot a couple of years ago.

"Whoa! That's like a golf cart limousine!" Jax said.

From the front, the cart resembled ones Delta had seen all over golf courses on Hilton Head. It had a nearly flat front, a roof held up by posts, and was open on the sides. Unlike one bench seat plus room for a couple of golf bags in the back, though, this cart seated at least six people in three rows. The first padded seat faced the steering wheel and plastic windshield, with the dashboard providing storage space and multiple cup holders. The second bench faced forward as well, while the third seat faced backward. Delta figured this cart wasn't intended for golfers at all, as there was no spot for storing golf bags.

"We're all headed to the Community Farm, right?" Jon asked.

"Yep, I'm showing them my goat, Bubba," Darius replied.

Jon slid behind the steering wheel, with Micah sitting beside him. Delta and Darius climbed onto the bench behind the older boys, leaving the rear-facing seat for Jax, who was still admiring the deluxe ride. Jon turned the keys in the ignition, and a slight purr signaled that the electric cart was ready to roll. Delta heard the crunch of gravel as the vehicle lurched forward.

"Hey! Wait for me!" Jax cried. "I wasn't on yet." The others turned in their seats and watched him walk across the parking lot toward them. Just as he was within reach of the cart, Jon stepped on the pedal again and drove another ten feet across the lot. Everyone in the cart burst out laughing.

"Haha. Very funny," Jax said with a smile, again walking in their direction.

"Sorry, man," Jon said. "I couldn't resist. Hop on."

Just as Jax started to step up onto the back seat of the cart, Jon lurched the vehicle forward one more time to resounding laughter. Well, all except Jax. This time, he ran to catch up with them, leapt into the seat, and clutched the armrest with both hands.

"Now you can go," he said, and off they went toward the dirt road at the end of the parking lot.

Delta and Darius soon found that they were holding on for dear life, too, firmly grasping the back of the seat in front of them. Unlike the paved roads they were used to on Hilton Head, Daufuskie was traversed by dirt roads rutted with potholes, some several inches deep. Riding down these roads was like bouncing along in an amusement park ride.

"This is awesome!" Jax shouted from the back seat as his sister squealed in delight.

"I'm not going that fast, but I can go slower," Jon offered.

"No!" came a resounding chorus from Delta, Jax, and Darius. Jon sped up—just a little—and everyone on the cart laughed and cheered.

The Daufuskie Community Farm was located in the center of the island, and Delta admired the view as they drove deeper into the interior. While Hilton Head was heavily wooded compared to her densely populated suburban neighborhood in Chicago, she was used to those trees being dotted with houses. Here on Daufuskie, though, there were just thick, jungly forests for what seemed like miles. Every so often, she would spy a pond or swampy area through the trees, but only occasionally did she see a house, usually made of wood and hosting a broad front porch. This area seemed way out in the country somewhere, and nothing about it indicated that you were on an island.

She knew they were headed in the right direction when she saw a street sign for the community farm, although it was unlike any street sign she had ever seen before. Periodically throughout their ride, they had encountered this island's version of an official marker: hand-painted wooden arrows nailed to tree trunks, each arrow indicating a certain location—"Church," "Lighthouse," "Gallery." This sign pointed the way to "Farm."

Jon turned a sharp left (causing them all to yell joyously as they clung to the cart for support) and pulled past a small wooden building with an open window spanning its front. Beneath the window were bins of late-season vegetables, including tomatoes, cucumbers, and potatoes. A handcrafted sign above the window read "Farmacy."

"Get it?" Jax laughed. "Like a drugstore, except they spell it with an 'F' like 'farm.'"

Jon pulled the cart to a stop and the group piled out.

"We'll find y'all after a while," Micah said, as he and Jon headed off to earn some community service points by volunteering at the facility. Meanwhile, the younger kids were free to explore the island's shared gardening and farming space.

"Bubba lives back this way," Darius said. They followed him down a mulched path that led between two areas the size of football fields. Each was surrounded by chain-length fences higher than Micah's head.

"That's to keep the critters out," Darius said. "The deer are especially bad at messing with gardens."

Delta noticed that one fenced area contained an orchard of fruit trees. She could see apples, lemons, and tangerines hanging heavy on the branches of some. Others were bare of fruit this time of year, but had signs at their bases indicating that they produced figs or peaches. She spied a family working in the orchard, but then realized she was seeing a quartet of scarecrows, two large and two small. One of each size was clad in a flannel shirt, denim overalls, and a straw hat. The remaining small one wore an old calico dress and a sun bonnet. The other large scarecrow, though, was decked out for Halloween in a black dress and a pointy black hat covering a bright orange mop of hair, a broomstick in her hand. *Is that how the islanders saw Constance True?* Delta wondered.

Opposite the orchard, the other fenced area protected dozens of plots filled with vegetables and flowers. Halfway across the field, a woman in a baseball cap knelt amidst rows of greenery, plucking weeds and tossing them in a yellowed sweetgrass basket. Delta noticed one patch filled with ripening orange pumpkins. Another resembled a patchwork quilt composed of mounds of daisies, asters, and mums in various shades of yellow, purple, and rusty red. Lined up across the back of this garden, like a row of townhouses, stood several wooden beehives, no doubt producing honey from the pollen of the nearby flowers.

"Hey, Uncle Rob!" Darius called.

Delta looked in the direction Darius was facing and did a double take. She knew Daufuskie was different, but had they been transported back in time, or to another world altogether?

20

Greeting the Goat

Once past the gardens, the community farm opened to what looked like a mixture between an old western ghost town and Munchkinland. Tiny wooden storefronts and farmhouses were interspersed with miniature barns and fenced corrals. Standing inside one paddock was a (normal-sized) bald man waving in their direction.

"There you are!" he said. "Bubba's been waiting on y'all!"

Darius and Jax took off at a run toward the corral, while Delta strolled along behind. She passed a playhouse-sized castle draped with an elaborate gold banner onto which was stitched "Prince Hamlet." The castle's drawbridge was open, allowing Delta to see inside. Lying atop what appeared to be a padded dog bed in the shade of his palace was the prince himself. The brown and white speckled hog blinked lazily at Delta as she passed by, unfazed by her chuckling.

Next, she came to an A-framed building, about the size of Pops's backyard shed, labeled *Poulet Chalet*. Two years of French class had taught her that meant *chicken house*, so she wasn't surprised to find a trio of multicolored hens puttering around their home. A loud *cock-a-doodle-doo* somewhere nearby hinted at a neighborhood rooster, as well.

"Here he is, Delta! Meet Bubba!" Delta peeked over the fence into the corral to find Darius hugging a tan goat with a black patch across its face. Jax stood beside them, stroking Bubba's back.

"He's real gentle," Jax said. "He just met me, and we're already friends."

Delta climbed the wooden fence and joined the others in the dirt paddock. "Hi," she said to the man who must be Darius's uncle. "I'm Delta Wells."

"And you can call me Uncle Rob," the man said, smiling.

"Oh, sorry," Darius said. "I should have introduced you. But it's been such a long time since I've seen Bubba! I used to visit him all the time when we kept the Tackies here, but now that they're on Hilton Head, we hardly ever make it over to Daufuskie."

"Our grandfather runs the Island History Museum, where Indy and Honey live now," Delta explained to Uncle Rob. "Visitors always love meeting them. Most have never even heard of Marsh Tackies."

"I imagine that's true, if they're not from the Carolinas," he said. "Tackies aren't especially big horses, but they're smart and relatively easy to take care of. Did you know they were originally left in these parts by Spanish explorers in the 1500s?"

Delta nodded. She did know that.

"They ran wild for a long time after that, and learned to pretty much fend for themselves, eating whatever they could find and surviving in the swamps and marshes."

"Yeah, we just learned that Colonel Francis Marion—the Swamp Fox—used Marsh Tackies to beat the British," Jax said.

Uncle Rob nodded. "Yep. Marion didn't have to haul food for his horses like the British did, because the Tackies just fed themselves as they went. Indy and Honey weren't the only ones here, you know." He motioned toward a larger barn in the distance. "There's a whole barn full of them over that way if you'd like to see them. I'm heading over there now."

"That'd be great," Delta said. "But first, I want to get to know Bubba better." As Uncle Rob headed toward the Tacky barn, she knelt down and tentatively reached toward the goat's back. Touching her fingertips to its fur, she was surprised to find it softer than she expected.

"So just how did you end up with a pet goat?" she asked her friend.

Darius sat cross-legged on the dirt, allowing room for his friends to play with Bubba. "Like I said, we used to come over here all the time. Uncle Rob and Auntie Joy live over here, so sometimes we'd come just to visit. But when our horses were here, we came a lot. Uncle Rob watched them for us every day, but Dad and I would come over at least a couple of times a week to help out."

"You're lucky your uncle owns this farm," Jax said. "It's really cool."

"It is cool," Darius said, "but Uncle Rob doesn't own it. It's the community farm, which means people all over the island can rent parts of it to use for gardening or to keep animals. Auntie Joy grows vegetables in one of the plots we passed, and Uncle Rob keeps some chickens here, and now he watches Bubba for me."

"And he said he has more Marsh Tackies," Delta said.

"No, those Tackies belong to someone else," Darius corrected, "but they don't mind people visiting them if they're careful. It's kind of one big family here on Daufuskie."

"Anyway, how'd you get Bubba?" Jax asked.

"Oh, right. So, there's this guy here who has goats. They live in a little house that looks like an Old West saloon over past the Tacky barn. One day a couple of years ago, I was here checking on Indy and Honey. Some new baby goats had been born, and their owner had them out in a little pen so people could see them."

"Aw, that must've been so cute!"

"It was, Delta. They were really little and awkward. But what caught my eye was this one baby goat that had its front legs in casts."

THE SEA WITCH'S REVENGE

"Casts?" Jax asked. "Like broken-leg casts?"

Darius nodded. "Apparently, when he was born, he just fell right out of his mama and landed on the ground on his front feet. Unfortunately, he landed wrong and broke both legs. The vet put casts on them so they'd heal properly or else he would have been crippled for life."

Delta glanced at the seemingly normal front legs of the goat she was currently cuddling. "And that little goat was Bubba? His legs were broken?"

"Yep. I kind of felt sorry for him that day, except he was such a happy little guy, trying to jump around like the other babies and never giving up. I really admired that about him."

Delta watched as Darius used an index finger to push his glasses farther up his nose, a habit he did without even noticing. By his own admission, Darius was nonathletic, generally quiet, and studious. He wasn't a kid that others often noticed, but Delta had come to know him as one of the kindest people she'd ever met. How like him to pick the one disabled goat and befriend him. Darius wouldn't hurt a fly, but he was being accused of vandalizing a cemetery? In fact, they were all pretty great kids, and yet it seemed that most people were quick to believe otherwise. Where was the justice in that? As she felt her anger rise, Delta resisted letting her thoughts stray back to that ugly topic.

"Bubba seems perfectly fine now," she said.

"He is. His owner saw how I took to him, and Bubba seemed to really like me, too. So, anyway, he said Bubba could be mine. He lives with the rest of his goat family, but Uncle Rob keeps an eye on him for me when I can't be around. I should come visit him more." Darius reached up and slung an arm around the goat's neck. Bubba nestled close to him, nuzzling the boy's chest.

Delta felt something wet drop on her head. Glancing up, she saw a murder of crows perched in the branches of a sprawling live oak tree directly above her.

Caw, caw! one bird announced.

Thanks, guys. Just what I needed today, she thought as she slowly reached to touch her hair. *As if this week hasn't been crappy enough.*

21

Racing the Rain

As it turned out, Delta had lucked out under the crows. Despite her worst fears, she discovered that she'd felt nothing more than a raindrop. But then that raindrop turned into a steady drip, leaving dark polka dots in the dirt of the corral. When a crack of thunder boomed through the farm, Darius spoke up.

"I thought your grandpa said it was going to be sunny here this afternoon?"

Jax shrugged. "Pops never claimed to be a weatherman!"

"Let's head to the Tacky barn," Darius said, gathering Bubba into his arms and taking off at a run as the shower turned into a deluge. Delta and Jax followed his lead, catching their breath once they entered the sanctuary of the dry barn. Darius placed Bubba on the dirt floor, where the goat proceeded to curl up and immediately go to sleep.

Jax shook his shaggy head like a wet dog, sprinkling the others with secondhand rain.

"Geez, Jax! Get a haircut!" Delta said.

Recovering from her wet run, she took a deep breath and inhaled the scents of drying hay, old wood, and fresh manure. Oddly, it didn't strike her as an especially bad smell. Empty horse stalls lined this spot just inside the barn door, but she could see the heads of two Marsh Tackies at the opposite end where Uncle Rob was standing.

"I'm real sorry to hear about that trouble over at the cemetery, Micah," he said.

From within one of the stalls, out of sight of the younger kids, Micah groaned. "Man, that news made it all the way over here?"

"Your mama told me about it. She's real upset and just needed to talk to her big brother is all."

"But you know I didn't do it, Uncle Rob, right? You know I would never do anything like that!"

"I believe you, son, but it's a mess of trouble, for sure. Were you there that night, too, Jon?"

From within another stall, Jon's voice rang out. "They invited me, but I had something else going on."

"I bet you're glad of that now," Micah said.

After a pause, Jon responded, "I just wish y'all hadn't gotten in so much trouble, that's all."

Just then, Uncle Rob looked up to see the younger kids approaching. Apparently, the pounding of rain on the barn roof had muffled their arrival.

"Well, look what the tide brought in!" he said with a laugh. "Y'all been swimming in the duck pond?"

"The weather around here is so weird," Jax said. "It can be perfectly clear and sunny one minute and storming out of nowhere the next."

Uncle Rob nodded. "It's because we're by the ocean. Storms blow in real fast, but then they don't usually last too long."

Delta reached out to pat the snout of a Tacky sticking its head out of the last stall in greeting. The stocky horse wasn't much taller than Delta, and it had a long flowing mane and sparkling eyes the size of quarters. Behind the horse, Micah was busy mucking the stall, tossing shovels of soiled straw into a wheelbarrow.

"What's this one's name?" Delta asked.

"This good girl is Miss Cotton," Uncle Rob told her, stroking the horse's mane. "She belongs to a neighbor of mine. Isn't she a pretty lady?"

"She sure is." Delta stared into the Tacky's friendly eyes.

Micah and Jon emerged from their respective stalls, each pushing filled wheelbarrows.

"We're pretty much done here for the day," Jon said. "The other stuff they wanted us to do is all outdoors, so that's not happening now with the rain."

"What time do you need to get back to Hilton Head, Delta?" Micah asked. "Darius mentioned you were going to a party tonight."

Her face reddened. "Yeah, well, those plans changed, so I don't have to be back by a certain time. But we would like to catch a bit of Tootsie's class at the museum if we can. It's supposed to be sometime late afternoon."

Jon pulled out his cellphone to check the time. "So, the next ferry leaves in about ninety minutes, so we have an hour or so to kill."

"I'd invite y'all over to our house, except Auntie Joy is hosting her book club today. She probably doesn't even want *me* there, let alone a pack of sopping kids." He smiled and winked.

"That's okay," Jon said. "We can go hang out at my house for a while until it's time for the ferry."

The group spent the next ten minutes visiting with the barn's resident Marsh Tackies until the rain seemed to slack off a bit. Uncle Rob promised to return Bubba to his own stall in the goat barn, while the kids ran at full speed in the direction of the parking lot.

"*Omigosh*! It's Prince Hamlet!" Delta cried. Rolling in a newly filled puddle in the now-muddy pathway was the giant speckled hog, fully enjoying the change in weather. Not far away, a family of domestic ducks splashed joyfully in a pond about the size of a child's wading pool. "I guess not everyone minds the rain!"

The kids piled onto the golf cart, realizing too late that the bench seats were all soaked. The cart buzzed as Jon backed up out of his parking space and then headed toward the wider dirt lane. When he pulled to an abrupt stop before entering the road, though, a wave of water washed over the edge of the cart's roof and landed right in Jax's lap.

"Hey!" Jax yelled, now thoroughly soaked from top to bottom.

"FYI," Jon said, "there are grooves on the roof of the cart that tend to collect water when it rains."

The others couldn't help but laugh, and Jax, ever the good sport, eventually joined in.

As they headed toward Jon's house, Delta noticed that what had been ruts and potholes on their ride to the community farm had now become muddy puddles of unknown depth. Jon swerved to avoid them, but the pools were so numerous that it was impossible to miss them all. One hole in particular was nearly a foot deep, and Delta wondered how they even managed to get through it. They were all completely wet and muddy by the time Jon turned a corner and drove onto a smooth, paved roadway.

"Welcome to Bloody Point!" he said.

22

Reaching the Point

"What the heck?" Jax called from the back seat.

Ahead, a carved stone sign read *"Bloody Point: A Private Residential Community."*

"His neighborhood is called Bloody Point?" Delta whispered to Darius. "Isn't that kind of gruesome?"

But Jon had heard her.

"This tip of the island has always been called Bloody Point, at least since, like, the 1700s. Apparently, there were a bunch of battles between the locals and the Yemassees, and loads of people were killed here. They say, 'the beach ran red with blood.'"

"Not creepy at all," Darius said, raising his eyebrows at Delta.

"Who were the Yemassees?" Jax asked.

"Some Native American tribe that lived around here, I guess," Jon said with a shrug. "I'm not personally that into history, but everybody asks about our neighborhood's name, so I've heard the story a hundred times."

"That's the Bloody Point Lighthouse," he added, motioning toward a white clapboard house with rocking chairs on the front porch.

"Where?" Delta strained to see a tall, cylinder-shaped building topped by a light, but there was none.

"That's it right there," Micah said, pointing again to the house. "The light was in that upstairs dormer window."

"Yeah, right," Jax said.

Jon and Micah laughed. "No, we're serious," Micah said. "The house used to be right by the beach, but they had to move it inland a bit because of erosion. I know it doesn't look like your typical lighthouse, but it did the job."

"So, it's literally a *light house*," Delta said.

Micah laughed. "Exactly! The keeper and his family lived right there, and just had to go to that window to turn on the light each night."

"Now that building is a museum," Jon said. "And the little room where the light used to be? After they stopped needing a lighthouse here, somebody bought the house and turned that room into a bathroom!"

"But it probably still has a light in it," Delta said.

"Yeah," Darius agreed, "but hopefully not one that shines for miles out at sea!"

The group rolled along the smooth asphalt, passing a manicured golf course and stately homes on spacious, neatly landscaped lawns.

"I thought you just had dirt roads on Daufuskie," Jax said.

Jon laughed. "Mostly. My neighborhood paid extra for these." He pulled into the driveway of a massive house and parked in a miniature garage just the right size for an extended-length golf cart. Before entering the house, though, Jon produced stacks of beach towels that the kids used to dry themselves as well as possible. They left their wet shoes and socks in a pile on the garage floor, peeled off their dripping jackets, and headed inside.

The first thing Delta noticed was the soaring ceilings. Jax could have stood on her head and still not reached the top of the kitchen cabinets. But then they entered the living room, which was nearly three stories high. The entire back wall was glass, looking out upon a kidney-shaped swimming pool surrounded by umbrella tables and chaise lounges. Palm trees and flowering shrubs surrounded the pool area, beyond which spread sand dunes and the Atlantic Ocean. It looked like a fancy island resort Delta had seen in magazines, except a family lived here all by themselves.

"What do Jon's parents do for a living?" Delta whispered to Darius while the older boys searched through the refrigerator for snacks. Jax had spread a dry towel on a leather ottoman by the window and plopped down beside them.

"They're both lawyers," Darius whispered back. "His dad actually represents some big-name pro athletes. In fact, a few summers ago, he had one of his clients, a defensive back from the Atlanta Falcons, visiting for a few weeks. The guy agreed to do some training with Jon, and Jon invited Micah to come join them. By the end of the summer, Micah had improved so much that he got to play on the varsity team as a sophomore."

"Wow," Jax said. "Did the training help Jon, too?"

"Oh, sure. They're both really good. Jon is kind of Micah's sidekick."

"So that makes Micah the superhero?" Delta grinned. "Seriously, though, I thought Daufuskie was a more rural island. I didn't expect to find a neighborhood like this one here."

"It's kind of a mix," Darius said. "A lot of Gullah families have been living here for generations, and there are some white families that have been here a long time, too. And then there are a couple of fancier areas like this one. Most of the people that own these houses on the beach just come a few weeks a year for vacation, or they rent them out. Jon's family is rare since they live here full time."

"Seems like kind of a waste to me," Delta said. "You know, to have beautiful houses with great views just sitting empty most of the time."

Darius shrugged. "Hey, not to change the subject, but did y'all notice that street sign we passed not long before we got to Bloody Point?"

"Which one?" Delta asked.

"It was one of those painted ones, but it said *Martinangel Road*. Why does that name sound so familiar?"

"Martinangel?" It sounded familiar to Delta, too, and then it came to her. "That's the name of Mrs. Talbird's brother-in-law! You know, the one who had her house burned down, but saved all of her furniture and stuff."

"That's right!" Darius said. "And he was a Tory from Daufuskie, wasn't he? Maybe he lived on that street."

Delta nodded. "That's so weird to think that he lived right here, maybe just a few blocks from where we're standing right now. With all our messages from Mercy, it's like time is all mixed together. Like Martinangel still lives there today, right by Bloody Point."

"Um, guys," Jax said, now standing, staring out the window. "Speaking of gruesome stuff that happened on this beach, look at that."

Delta followed her brother's gaze and gasped. Lying on the sand, on the edge of the breaking surf, was a beached dolphin.

23

Dining with Dolphins

The rain had slowed to a drizzle by the time the kids raced across the dunes to rescue the stranded dolphin. Jax was in the lead, with the other four not far behind.

"How can we move it back into the water?" Delta asked. "Don't dolphins weight hundreds of pounds?"

"I'm not even sure we're supposed to move it," Darius said. "What if we hurt it or something?"

"Who are we supposed to call to help with wildlife?" Micah asked. "Should we just call the sheriff's office?"

Everyone had questions, but no one had any answers.

When the four older kids crested the last dune, though, they could see Jax standing in the surf alone.

"It's gone," he said. "It was already gone when I got here."

"That's good, right?" Delta bent over, her hands on her knees, catching her breath. "At least it's not stranded anymore."

"So, this is Bloody Point?" Jax asked, and Jon nodded.

Looking southward, Delta could see a wide swath of sand wrap around the end of Dawfuskie Island. "Is that where those Native

American attacks happened?"

"Yeah," Jon replied, "but it wasn't just them attacking the islanders. Sometimes, it was the other way around."

"How did that happen? Did the Yemassees live here, too?"

"I guess they did before the British came," Jon said, "but not by the 1700s. The water that meets the ocean here is the Intracoastal Waterway, sort of a protected highway for boats to use, traveling down the coast without having to be out in the ocean. The Yemassees used the waterway to sneak north and attack Port Royal so the British would catch them on the way back south. They'd hide in the dunes here and wait for canoes to come around the bend. When they did . . . BANG! They'd get 'em."

"Yikes," Jax said.

"But then the Yemassee came to count on the islanders to be waiting for them there, so one time they snuck up somehow and caught the islanders in the dunes and slaughtered them. Beat 'em at their own game. This went back and forth for years."

"Sounds like they were all out for revenge," Delta said. Between this story, the Sea Witch, Mercy's militia tales, and their own cemetery woes, talk of revenge seemed to be everywhere these days.

Suddenly, though, her thoughts were interrupted by a shout from her brother.

"It's back! And it brought friends!"

Delta spun to see four dolphins seemingly riding the waves directly toward shore. Their noses in the water, their fins rose above the breaking surf as they neared the beach.

"They shouldn't be coming this close, should they?" she said. "What if they all get stranded?"

The animals swam purposefully forward, sometimes turning sideways but always together. In front of them, the water roiled and splashed.

"Oh! I know what's happening!" Jon said. "It's kind of a peculiarity of dolphins around here."

"But won't they get hurt?" Jax asked.

Suddenly, all four dolphins leapt forward onto the shore, causing all five kids to jump backwards away from them.

"Whoa! I've heard of this, but I've never seen it before," Darius said.

"Neither have I," Micah agreed.

Directly in front of the dolphins, six-inch-long fish flopped frantically on the sand. One by one, the dolphins snatched the fish and swallowed them all. Then, with a jerk of their tails, the mammals slid back into the waters where the Atlantic Ocean and Intracoastal Waterway met.

"What is happening?" Delta asked. She watched as the dolphins swam back to deeper water and then circled back to head toward shore again.

"It's called strand feeding," Darius explained. "For some reason, dolphins have only been seen doing it around the Carolinas and Georgia. Normally, bottlenose dolphins fish alone, but around here, they sometimes work as a group. They kind of *herd* a school of fish onto shore and then grab them."

Now that she knew what she was looking for, Delta could see a school of panicked fish splashing in front of the determined dolphins. Once again, the quartet herded their quarry to shore and feasted before sliding gracefully back into the water.

"So that first dolphin I saw wasn't really stranded?" Jax asked.

"Nope. It's the fish that get stranded," Micah said. "The dolphins are just fine."

The kids stood for a few moments longer, watching the curious feeding ritual. The dolphins' long mouths seemed to grin, and their squeaks indicated the joy they found in the activity.

Is that how it was for the islanders when they defeated their Native American foes on this very spot? Delta wondered. *And then, when the Yemassee got their revenge at Bloody Point, were they joyful? Did it make up for their previous losses, seeing 'the beach running red with blood'?*

The "limo cart" (as Jax had begun calling it) pulled into the parking lot at the Daufuskie ferry terminal with about thirty minutes to spare. The sun was again shining, the sky again as clear and blue as if it had never rained at all.

"Let's sit in the sun on the dock so our clothes can finish drying out," Darius suggested. The three younger kids headed toward the awaiting benches.

"Surprise, surprise," a vaguely familiar voice said. "So, they let you off Hilton Head, did they? Or are you just escaping from the law over here?"

"Hey, Waldo," Micah said, choosing to ignore his teammate's remarks.

Jon nodded at Waldo. "Hey, man."

"Look who it is!" Delta whispered to Jax and Darius.

"Our prime suspect," Jax replied, and then stomped over toward the older boys. "What are you doing here?" he asked, his hands on his hips.

Waldo sneered down at him. "I live here, you little toad. What's your excuse?"

"Where were you on the night of October . . . October . . . last Sunday night?" Jax replied, clearly forgetting the date.

"And just why is that any of your business? Did something criminal happen that night, perhaps at the Zion Cemetery?" Waldo asked. "I'm not the one the sheriff is after, so leave me out of it." He headed down the dock and stepped into a small motorboat. As he put the key into the ignition, he shouted up at Micah and Jon.

"Hey! Did you hear the good news? Looks like I'm gonna be the team kicker again."

Jon and Micah exchanged a confused look. "How's that supposed to happen?" Jon asked.

"Coach told me your little friend Ivy is getting shipped off to military school by her parents, so I'm back in business. See ya at practice!" He turned away, laughing, and sped across Calibogue Sound.

"That's not true, is it?" Jon asked Micah.

Micah scowled. "I sure hope not. Ivy's dad took her phone away, so I haven't been able to talk to her all week. Last I heard, her parents were *really* mad, though."

"Man, that's tough," Jon said, watching Waldo speed out of sight. "I guess this thing at the cemetery has really blown up, huh? I mean, who'd have thought it would cause so much trouble?"

Jax returned to where Delta and Darius were sitting. "In answer to my earlier question, I believe we *do* have an enemy on Daufuskie Island," he said.

"I think you may be right," Darius said, nodding toward the edge of the dock. Not far from where Waldo's boat had just been, several wooden crates were neatly stacked. One box sat open on the ground, revealing its contents: cans of florescent orange spray paint.

24

Spying the Massacre

Oyster shells crunched beneath them as Micah drove his mom's old car up the curving lane toward the Island History Museum. Delta always loved this view, with loblolly pines and draping live oaks circling the swaying meadows where Sea Island cotton, rice, and indigo had once grown in abundance. Micah dropped Darius at the horse barn in the meadow so he could check on Indigo and Honey, and then continued down the lane.

"Thanks for the ride from the ferry terminal, Micah," Delta said. "I hope it wasn't out of your way."

"Not a problem," he said. He had hardly spoken a word since they'd boarded the ferry on Daufuskie. Waldo's news about Ivy going to military school had clearly gotten to him.

Maybe Waldo just made that up to get a rise out of Micah, Delta thought. After all, here's what they knew about Waldo: First, he was mad at Micah and Ivy about the football team. Second, he had access to paint for tagging the mausoleum. Third, he had helped spread the news that they were guilty of the crime. Fourth, he was taking great pleasure in their being in trouble. Clearly, Waldo could not be trusted to tell the truth about anything.

Delta fought back her rising anger by staring at the comfortably familiar scene out the car window. Dogwoods and crepe myrtles dotted the grounds, now trading their blossoms for leaves of orange, gold, and crimson. Around a cluster of magnolia trees, the old plantation house that now served as the museum's main building came into view. A few visitors sat in rocking chairs on the wide front porch, while a group of about a dozen men, women, and children stood in a semicircle in the front yard. As the car pulled closer, Delta saw that they were all watching a demonstration of some kind.

"Hey! There's Tootsie!" Jax said. After thanking Micah again, the siblings climbed out and hurried to catch the last of their grandmother's papermaking class.

"Be sure to fill the blender about halfway with water first, but then drop in your recyclables," Tootsie was saying. Beside her on a folding table was a pile of what looked like newspapers torn into thumb-sized pieces. She flipped a switch and the appliance whirred loudly. "Keep it mixing until it's a thick liquid, and then pour it on your screen," she shouted over the noise of the blender.

"That's the grossest-looking smoothie I've ever seen," Jax told his sister, grinning as their grandmother tipped the pitcher.

A gray glop ran out onto a wooden tray lying on the table. When Tootsie lifted the tray, the kids could see that, although the sides were made of wood, the bottom was a metal screen. As Tootsie stepped away from the table and shook the tray from side to side, the glop spread out, and murky water dripped onto the grass below.

"See?" she said to the surrounding spectators. "What's left is just pulp." She tilted the tray slightly to show a layer of gray mush covering most of the screen. "After a few days of drying, you can peel off your own homemade paper, like the samples I showed you earlier."

A murmur spread through the gathered crowd, followed by applause.

Jax giggled. "They're probably telling each other it'd just be easier to use store-bought paper."

Delta rolled her eyes. "It's a craft, Jax. The point isn't to be easy. Sometimes it's just fun to make stuff." She led her brother to the table where their grandmother was wiping the outside of the blender with a rag.

"Hey there, sweeties!" Tootsie said. "I'd give you both hugs, except I'm covered in wet pulp." She dried her hands on the rag, which looked suspiciously like one of Pops's old white T-shirts. "Delta, would you mind gathering up my paper samples so I don't ruin them?"

"Sure, Tootsie." She began to stack the dozen or so sheets displayed on the opposite end of the long table. "I never knew there were so many different kinds of paper." Each sample was unique, varying in texture and weight, with some speckled and some solid in color.

"Before I started the demonstration, I talked about the history of paper," Tootsie told them. "It's been made different ways over the centuries as technology has developed. This piece here, for example, was used a couple of hundred years ago. It's made from cotton fibers instead of wood pulp like we generally use today."

Delta examined the delicate sheet her grandmother had indicated, a bit rougher to the touch than the modern-day paper Delta and Jax used in school, and of a heavier weight. This piece had yellowed some with age, and Delta could see the similarities between it and the pages of Mercy's journal.

"Those samples can go in the folder in my tote bag there," Tootsie said, nodding toward a satchel on the ground behind the table.

Delta pulled a stiff cardboard folder from the tote bag and carefully slid the stack she had gathered into it. If some of these papers were hundreds of years old, they needed to be handled with care. She replaced the folder and turned back toward her grandmother.

"I'll go wash out the blender and the tray if you can take these extra newspapers to the storage room," Tootsie was saying. "I'll save them to use for my next class."

"I can go put your bag in Pops's office," Jax offered.

"Great idea, Jax!" Tootsie said. "Oh! I forgot to tell you at lunch, we got an email from your parents. They wanted you to know they're doing well but were headed back out to a remote area. They said they'll be in a more developed area next week and will call then. Won't it be great to hear their voices?"

"It sure will, Tootsie," Jax said without enthusiasm. He and Delta exchanged a worried glance. There'd likely be angry voices once Mom and Dad heard about the cemetery trouble.

Delta's heart sunk as she gathered an armful of stacked newspapers. Sure, she missed seeing and talking to her parents while they worked on the other side of the world. What she hated even more than being away from them, though, was the thought of disappointing them. By this time next week, Mom and Dad would likely know all about the mess their kids were in. What would happen then? Would Delta and Jax have to go to boarding school like Ivy's parents had threatened? Would they have to go live on the Siberian tundra with Mom and Dad? It'd be great to see them, but not there. Even Tootsie and Pops had agreed on that.

Climbing the steps to the museum, Delta's shoulders slumped as she passed through the front lobby and down the hall. Each room of the old house served a new purpose now, filled with exhibits on the island's flora and fauna, as well as various eras in Hilton Head's history. What had once served as a pantry near the back door was now the storage room where the kids had first discovered the Crazy Box. Delta stacked Tootsie's craft materials on an empty shelf in the dimly-lit room and headed back into the exhibit area.

She had been through all of these rooms a hundred times. She and Jax had played hide-and-seek in them on days when visitors were few, and they had helped dust and vacuum the old house countless times over the years. Jax preferred the hands-on displays, particularly the skeletons and pelts in the Lowcountry Critters room, but even he occasionally appreciated reading the informational posters and maps. Delta, though, fully believed she had examined every single exhibit in her grandfather's museum.

How did I miss this one? she thought, as she did a double take in what used to be a grand dining room.

Before her hung a shadowbox display titled *The Muster House Massacre of 1781.*

"Jax! Where are you?" Delta called. Her brother had come in the front door right behind her, so he must be inside somewhere. He had to see this. "Jax!"

A man pushing a stroller containing a sleeping toddler turned toward Delta with his finger to his lips.

"Sorry!" Delta whispered. She rounded the corner into the Lowcountry Critter room, then stuck her head into the former living room hung with local works of art. She finally found Jax sitting on a beanbag chair in the museum bookstore, paging through a children's picture book about pirates.

"Jax! You won't believe what I found! Come look!" She grabbed him by the hand and jerked him up out of the bean bag. After tossing the pirate book onto the seat, he followed her down the hall and to the new discovery.

"Look at this!" Delta said. The man with the stroller had moved on to the next room, so she read aloud: "Hearing rumors of a planned attack on their island, the Daufuskie Royal Militia led a raiding party to Hilton Head and ambushed the Patriots at the Militia Muster House *near the present-day Zion Cemetery.*"

"No way!" Jax said. "That place was trouble for us, too!"

Delta pulled out her phone and typed in "Muster House." She'd had no internet connection when she'd searched for the term on their camping trip, but the museum had Wi-Fi. "It says here that a *muster house* was a building where troops assembled for inspection or to prepare for battle."

"So, like the militia's clubhouse?" Jax asked.

Delta shrugged. "Sort of, I guess. And the one here was next to the Zion Cemetery. See, here's a map."

The drawing showed a close-up of the northern part of Hilton Head Island, centering on the current Zion Cemetery. Next to the graveyard was a red dot denoting where the muster house had been, and not far from that was a black dot labeled *Two Oaks Plantation*.

"That's where Mercy lives," Jax said.

Delta nodded, but then pointed to a blue section on the map, adjacent to the cemetery site. "I didn't realize Broad Creek came up this far," she said. "Did you notice that Zion backed up to the marsh?"

Jax shook his head. "It was too dark to see when we were there. But this dotted line on the water leads all the way from Daufuskie. It looks like the Royal Militia guys snuck up the creek. See, look at this boat."

In the bottom of the shadowbox sat a wooden model, a miniature reproduction of a flat-bottomed eighteenth-century rowboat. Delta could imagine Tories using similar vessels, gliding silently through the darkness on an October night 250 years ago. Unsuspected by the Patriots on shore, they could have beached their boats in the marsh, then struck without warning.

"Did you read this part?" Jax pointed to the next paragraph on the written display. "It says the Daufuskie ambush was led by British Major Anthony Maxwell and Loyalist Captain *Philip Martinangel*. That's Mrs. Talbird's brother-in-law, right? The one who saved her furniture. Maybe he wasn't such a nice guy, after all."

Delta shook her head. "Wow. I mean, he had family on Hilton Head, but they were his enemies, too, I guess." She read the poster further. "Surprised by the attack during a planning meeting, *every member* of the Patriot militia was killed. This bloody massacre could have changed the face of the revolution in the South, except that news arrived *several weeks later* announcing the war's end. General Charles Cornwallis had surrendered to Colonel George Washington at Yorktown on October 19, effectively ending the Revolutionary War."

"Hold on," Jax said. "When did this ambush at the Mustard House take place?"

"*Muster* house," Delta corrected, searching the exhibit for a date. "October 22, 1781. So, three days *after* the war had ended." She paused to let that sink in. "They hadn't heard the news yet down here on the Sea Islands, so they just kept fighting. The whole militia on Hilton Head died for nothing."

"Even Mercy's dad," Jax added, then opened his eyes wide. "Wait a second!" He ran to the front of the building and returned with his backpack. Digging in it, he pulled out Mercy's journal. Flipping frantically through the pages, he found the latest entry and jabbed a finger at the top of the page.

"Mercy wrote this yesterday—on October 20. Her dad is going to die in less than two days, Delta! We have to warn her!"

25

Sending a Warning

As soon as the dinner dishes were cleared that night, Tootsie and Pops settled in the living room to watch a documentary on television. Delta and Jax retreated to her room to discuss the situation at hand.

"We can't just sit here doing nothing, knowing that our friend's dad is going to be killed!" Jax insisted.

Delta frowned. "She's not exactly our friend. I mean, we've never actually met her. We've just read her diary."

This time, Jax rolled his eyes. "Well, she feels like a friend to *me*! And even if we've never met her, wouldn't you want someone—even a stranger—to warn us if our dad was going to die?"

"Don't even say that, Jax! That's terrible!"

"I know it is. And it's going to be terrible for Mercy in a couple of days, too, if we don't do something to stop it."

Delta considered this. "But what if we *can't* stop it? Like Darius said the other day, 'the past is the past.' Is it even possible to change history?"

"We've got to at least try!" Jax looked close to tears. "This is really, really important, Delta."

She sighed. She had to agree that she'd feel guilty if they didn't even attempt to warn Mercy about the upcoming ambush at the Muster House.

"So, how do we do it?" she asked.

"I've been thinking about it ever since this afternoon," Jax said. "You know how Mercy always writes to her Guardian Angel?"

Delta nodded.

"I say we write her a note pretending to be the angel. You know, like sending her a response. 'Sorry I didn't write back sooner . . . blah, blah, blah. By the way, don't let your dad go to the mustard house.' What do you think?"

"Maybe not those exact words," Delta said. "But that might work."

Jax ran across the hall to his own room and returned shortly with a spiral notebook and blue ballpoint pen. He climbed onto Delta's bed, flipped the notebook open, and began to write.

"Dear Mercy," he spoke aloud as he wrote. "I am your Guardian Angel. How are you? I am fine."

"That's not what a Guardian Angel would say," Delta said, grabbing the notebook and pen from her brother. She scratched out everything he'd written so far. "How about this?"

"My dearest Mercy," she cleared her throat and stared at the ceiling in thought. Finally, she began to write again, speaking as the blue pen scratched across the lined paper. "As it is a Guardian Angel's duty to watch over and protect his or her charge, I feel compelled to warn you of an upcoming danger to your family."

"Ooh! That's good!" Jax said.

The duo spent the next twenty minutes writing and rewriting the rest of their letter to Mercy. When they finally felt satisfied with the completed letter, Delta tore the page from the spiral and handed it to her brother.

"Perfect! I'll stick it in the next blank page of the journal and put the book in the Crazy Box for Mercy," Jax said.

"Wait, you goofwad! You can't put it in the box like that!"

"Why not?" Jax looked at the 8-1/2 inch by 11 inch page in his hand. "I'll fold it in half."

"No, it's not the size. It's the paper," Delta said. "They didn't have blue-lined, three-hole-punched paper 250 years ago. What would Mercy think of that?"

Jax glanced again at the paper he was holding, a fringe of torn nubs dangling from its side where Delta had torn it from the spiral notebook. "Maybe Guardian Angel paper is different," he suggested. "I mean, nobody really knows what kind of paper they use in heaven."

Delta laughed. "Yeah, *no!* Tootsie has a gazillion different kinds of paper around here. Surely we can find something better for our final draft."

Until a few months ago when Delta and Jax had come to stay with their grandparents, Delta's bedroom had served as Tootsie's art studio. Most of her supplies had been moved to make space for Delta's own belongings, but some were still stored on the top shelf of the closet. In fact, Pops had climbed on her desk chair just before dinner to reach that very shelf. Delta had watched him put the paper samples from Tootsie's class in a box up there. She pulled the chair across the room and opened the closet door.

Unfortunately, though, she was about a foot shorter than her grandfather.

"That shelf is still too high for me," she groaned.

"Let me try," Jax said, trying to shove her off the chair.

"You're shorter than I am," Delta said. "What good would that do?"

"Maybe my arms are longer than yours."

"You'd have to have arms like an ape to reach that box," Delta told him. "We need something taller to stand on."

Jax glanced around the room. "How about the desk?"

It took them nearly ten minutes to carefully slide the piece of furniture to the closet. It wasn't a huge desk, but it was surprisingly heavy and did not want to slide easily over the plush carpeting in the bedroom. Once in place, though, it was just the right height for Delta to reach the top shelf of her closet. She lifted the box of papers and handed it down to her brother waiting below.

"We should use that cotton paper Tootsie showed us," Jax said. "It's from around Mercy's time."

Delta hesitated. "I don't know. If it's that old, it's probably really expensive. And Tootsie uses it for her classes. I wouldn't feel right taking it."

They searched through the box, taking care not to bend any of the samples.

"This one might work." Delta lifted a thick sheet of tan parchment. The texture was fairly smooth, but its inconsistent color was darker in some areas than others. It looked old-timey, somehow, and would be the next-best-thing to the old cotton paper. Leaving the desk where it was, she pulled up the chair, sat, and prepared to copy their letter.

"Hold on!" Jax said. "Mercy never uses blue ink."

Delta looked at the ballpoint pen in her hand. "Duh. What was I thinking?" She dug through her desk drawer and pulled out a black gel pen. "This should be okay. I wish Darius was here to write in cursive, but I'll use my best printing."

"Maybe Guardian Angels don't use cursive."

"Well, this one doesn't," Delta said, and then she wrote their message to Mercy.

My Dearest Mercy,

As it is a Guardian Angel's duty to watch over and protect his or her charge, I feel compelled to warn you of an upcoming danger to your family.

You confided in me that the Hilton Head Patriots plan to meet at the Muster House on the evening of October 22 to plan their revenge on the Tories from Daufuskie Island. DO NOT LET THIS MEETING HAPPEN! The Tories intend to ambush the Patriots at the Muster House during that meeting and spare NO lives!

You must warn your father! This is a matter of LIFE AND DEATH!

Your loving protector, GA

Delta folded the parchment in thirds and handed it to her brother. Still hearing the television in the living room, they slipped across the hall into Jax's room. He pulled Mercy's journal from his backpack, tucked their letter inside like a bookmark, and placed it in the Crazy Box.

"Now, we just wait until tomorrow, I guess," Delta said.

Jax nodded. "Do you think she'll believe us that the Tories are going to attack?"

"I hope so," Delta said. "But even if she warns her father, will he believe *her*?"

26

Mending the Past

"The Crazy Box is gone!"

Delta awoke the next morning to her brother's frantic voice. She opened her eyes a slit and saw Jax standing over her, bouncing nervously.

"It's probably just hiding under one of your piles of dirty clothes," she told him. "Clean your room."

"No, it's not in there," he said, pacing the floor. "I couldn't get to sleep last night because I was so nervous about Mercy, and then I decided to leave her another gift in the box—a nice one this time—since I felt so bad about scaring her with the fox fur."

Delta sat up in bed as Jax continued.

"There wasn't anything interesting in my room . . ."

"Nothing you could find in all that mess, you mean," Delta interrupted.

Jax pretended he hadn't heard her. "So, I took the box into the living room to see what I could find there. Tootsie has that big bowl of sea glass sitting on the coffee table, and I didn't think she'd mind if I gave Mercy just one piece of it. I picked a really pretty blue chunk . . ."

Delta yawned. "I'm sure Mercy will love it."

"Anyway," Jax continued, "I went in the kitchen to get a snack. Did you know that cold macaroni and cheese is even better than when it's hot?"

"*Omigosh*! What does this have to do with the Crazy Box?"

"I was eating the mac and cheese and Pops must've heard me, because he showed up and told me to get back to bed. He walked me back to my room, and I guess I left the box on the coffee table."

"So?" Delta said. "It's somewhere in the living room then. Maybe Tootsie moved it to dust or something."

"No!" Jax said. "I've looked everywhere for it, and it's gone! I asked Tootsie if she'd seen it and she said, 'What box is that?' She didn't even know what I was talking about. We've got to find out if Mercy got our message last night!"

In her half-sleeping state, Delta had forgotten about the letter of warning they'd sent. Now she was wide awake. "How about Pops? Has he left for work yet?"

"I haven't seen him," Jax said.

Delta shooed her brother from her room and quickly changed from pajamas into a pair of jeans and a T-shirt. Pulling on her sneakers, she hurried into the kitchen where Tootsie was pouring herself a cup of coffee.

"Is Pops still around?" Delta asked.

Her grandmother raised her eyebrows. "Well, good morning to you, too!"

"Sorry, Tootsie, but I really need to ask Pops something. Has he already headed to the museum?"

Tootsie cradled the warm mug in both hands, inhaling the rising steam. "Not just yet. I heard him banging on something in the garage," she said.

Delta rushed into the garage to find her grandfather huddled over his workbench.

"What are you working on, Pops?" she asked.

He turned toward her and smiled. "Just doing a little fix-'em-up is all. I noticed that old box you kiddos found at the museum had some weak spots, so I rehabbed it for you. See? New and improved!" He motioned to the workbench and Delta's eyes grew wide.

Apparently, the project on the table used to be the Crazy Box, but it was hardly recognizable now.

"I put some metal hinges on it instead of those old worn leather pieces. And I replaced those two rotting boards with new ones," Pops explained proudly. "I had some weathered wood, so it blends in okay. Don't you think so?"

To Delta's eye, the old and new woods did not blend at all. It was obvious that at least half of the box had been replaced. She stepped forward to examine it more closely and gasped. "Pops, the board with the initials carved on it is gone now!"

"It was one that needed replacing," Pops said, sounding less enthusiastic now that he sensed Delta's disappointment. "I thought you'd be pleased."

The door from the house burst open and Jax stepped into the garage. Seeing the "new and improved" Crazy Box, he pretty much went ballistic.

"What have you done, Pops? Where's all our stuff?"

"Now, calm down, Jackson. I didn't bother anything you were keeping in the box. See? I placed it all on this shelf for safe keeping. You can put it back in the original box now if you'd like."

"But it isn't the original box anymore!" Jax whined.

Delta searched through the items on the shelf to find a pile of tiny acorns, a toy soldier, a clump of fox fur, a piece of blue sea glass, and a folded sheet of parchment. "Pops, what did you do with the journal?"

"Journal?" Pops scowled. "There wasn't any journal in there. This is everything that was in the box when I found it."

Delta and Jax exchanged a panicked look.

"I'm sorry if I did something I shouldn't have," Pops said, "but I have to say, you kiddos seem to be overreacting a bit. I thought you'd be happy to have your old box fixed up."

"Um, sure, Pops. No problem. We were just surprised is all," Delta said. How could they explain to him the importance of the Crazy Box? He'd never believe them.

Jax placed all of Mercy's gifts—and their letter to her—in the now strangely unfamiliar chest and carried it glumly back into the house. He and Delta conferred in his room.

"Are you absolutely sure you put the journal in there last night?" she asked, plopping down hard on Jax's unmade bed.

"Positive!"

"And you didn't take it back out later, like when you added the sea glass?"

"Why would I have taken it back out?" Jax asked. "And anyway, our letter was tucked inside the journal. The letter is still here!"

Delta's heart sank. "You don't think that means Mercy never saw our message, do you?"

Jax shrugged. "I hope it doesn't mean that. She has to warn her dad about the Tories attacking the Mustard House!"

"Muster," Delta corrected, considering what her brother had just said. She pulled her cell phone from her jeans pocket and placed a call.

"Meet us in an hour," she said. "I know how Waldo snuck into the cemetery last Sunday night."

27

Going by Gravestones

By the light of day, the Zion Cemetery didn't seem nearly as ominous as it had during their lantern-lit storytelling session. Delta and Jax parked their bikes in the rack on the edge of the parking lot and approached the gate in the old iron fence. Lifting the heavy latch, Delta swung the gate open and stepped into the resting place of the island's former inhabitants.

"It's actually kind of peaceful here," Jax said.

Delta nodded. "I was just thinking that."

Nestled beneath a cluster of live oak trees, an oyster shell path wound through an assortment of stone markers, many so heavily weathered from age that the inscriptions on them were nearly illegible. Larger brick monuments sprung up here and there, perhaps memorializing those of exceptional importance or wealth. Filtered sunlight dappled the ground below, highlighting the occasional orange or red leaf fallen from the crepe myrtle trees that adorned the cemetery with sherbet-colored blossoms throughout the summer and into the early fall.

Delta and Jax followed the crunching path until they arrived at what appeared to be a small house carved from stone. A canopy of

Spanish moss hung from twisting oak branches overhead, dangling toward the words *Integrity and Uprightness* carved over the door. Inside the mausoleum, they knew, lay multiple generations of the Baynard family, community leaders on Hilton Head for hundreds of years.

"It's a wonder that many people can fit in there," Delta said. "I mean, the building's about the size of Pops's backyard shed, and we're talking dozens and dozens of dead Baynards."

"Pops told me there are shelves in there for the coffins. He said they would leave each dead body in its coffin for a year or so, until it was completely decomposed and started to fall apart. Then they'd take the skeleton out and dump it in a section on the bottom with all the older bones. It saved space that way."

Delta gagged. "Gross!"

"Yeah, but then it cleared a spot on the shelf for the next new dead person."

Mentally trapped in images of skeleton piles, Delta jumped when she felt a tap on her shoulder.

"It's just me." Darius laughed. "Why are you so surprised? You told me to meet you here."

She grabbed her friend's arm. "We've got so much to tell you!" She pulled him toward a nearby bench and motioned for him to sit with her. Jax was too excited to stay still.

"Pops ruined the Crazy Box!" he said, pacing back and forth in front of the bench. "And the journal is gone, but our letter was still there!"

Darius turned to Delta. "What is he talking about?"

"You're getting ahead of the story, Jax," she said.

Her brother nodded and took a deep breath. "You tell it, Delta. I'm too worked up."

"Okay, I guess we should start by explaining that we saw a display at the museum about the ambush at the Muster House. Remember how we'd seen somewhere earlier that the Tories killed the entire Hilton

Head militia?"

Darius nodded. "Yeah, I think we saw that online somewhere."

"Well, the exhibit at the museum said that ambush happened on October 22—just two days after Mercy's last journal entry!"

"Wow, that's soon."

"Exactly! So, we couldn't just have that information and not warn Mercy that her dad was about to be killed, right? We had to do something."

"Like what?" Darius asked, staring back and forth between his friends.

"We wrote her a letter," Jax said. "We pretended to be that Guardian Angel she's always writing to, and we warned her to stop the militia meeting at the Mustard House."

"You did what?" Darius leapt to his feet. "What were you thinking?"

"We told you," Delta said, startled by his reaction. "We wanted to help Mercy save her dad's life. Wouldn't you want to know in advance if you could stop something terrible from happening to your parents?"

"Well, sure, but what happened to Mercy's dad *has already happened*! He was killed almost 250 years ago! You can't change the past!"

"But, to Mercy, it's still the future—barely. Maybe she *can* change it."

"You're not getting it, Jax. Even if you *could* change something in the past, or get Mercy to change it, that doesn't mean you *should*. Haven't you heard of the *butterfly effect*?"

"What's any of this got to do with butterflies?" Jax said.

"No, I've heard of that," Delta said. "That's the theory that if you change even one tiny thing in the present, it can cause huge differences in the future—like a butterfly fluttering its wings today can lead to a tornado a month later."

"That's crazy talk," Jax said, rolling his eyes. "Butterflies don't cause tornadoes."

Delta shrugged. "I'm probably explaining it wrong."

"The point is," Darius continued, "if Mercy warns her dad and changes the past, our present could turn out to be totally different."

Delta and Jax pondered this. They hadn't considered the long-term ramifications of sending that letter. They'd just wanted to save their friend some heartache.

"My dad showed me this old movie," Darius said. "A teenager manages to go back in time to when his parents were in high school. He meets them, but then accidently prevents them from falling in love. As a result, they never get married and he's never even born!"

"Well, we're still here," Jax said.

Darius sighed. "I'm just saying it was a really risky thing you did. Who knows what you might have changed?"

"But that's just it," Delta said. "We're not even sure that Mercy saw our letter. We left it in her journal last night, but this morning Pops had dismantled the Crazy Box and rebuilt it with new parts. He even replaced the board that Mercy had carved her initials into. All the stuff we had put into the box—including our letter—was there, but the journal had completely disappeared."

Darius pushed his glasses farther up his nose. "So, you're saying that only the modern-day stuff stayed? Not the 1781 book?"

Delta and Jax both nodded.

Darius sighed. "You know how we figured the old wood from the Talbird Oak plus the new acorns from the same tree created some kind of time connection? I hate to tell y'all this, but it sounds like your grandpa may have busted your magic box."

"That's what I was thinking, too," Delta said.

Jax shook his head. "Well, I'm not ready to give up yet. Maybe Mercy's journal will be back in the box tomorrow. Maybe she just forgot to put it in there this time because she was busy warning her dad about the Tories sneaking up Broad Creek."

"Oh!" Delta shouted, grabbing Darius by the arm again. "I almost forgot—that's the other reason we needed to talk to you. Did you know that this very cemetery backs up to Broad Creek?"

"It does?" Darius glanced around the graveyard, seeing nothing but foliage on two sides, with the parking lot and main road abutting the other two sides. "Where's the creek?"

"The museum exhibit had a map showing how the Tories from Daufuskie rowed their boats up Broad Creek all the way to the Muster House. Apparently, the Muster House stood about where we parked our bikes over there." She pointed toward the parking lot. "That means the creek is just through those woods behind the mausoleum."

"Okay . . ." Darius clearly wasn't seeing the connection to their modern-day troubles.

"Waldo is a Daufuskie Tory, and he brought his boat over here to ambush us at the Mustard House!" Jax said. "He snuck into the cemetery from the water. That's why no other cars showed up on the parking lot camera."

Darius's eyes grew wide. "Would that have been possible?"

"Let's go check it out," Delta said.

The trio headed around the corner of the mausoleum and walked directly into a strip of yellow caution tape stretched between the building and a nearby tree.

"Police tape," Jax said. Ironically, although they'd come to this spot to prove their innocence, it hadn't seemed much like a crime scene on this sunny autumn day. Not until now.

The kids stared at the smooth stone wall behind the tape. Neon paint the color of the Sea Witch's hair defaced the historic crypt. *IHS Sharks*, the lettering said, followed by Micah's initials.

Glancing around the nearby graves, the kids noticed multiple toppled tombstones, also marked by yellow tape. Not far away, more tape roped off a wrought-iron fence surrounding a statue of an angel. Several rails of the antique barrier were badly bent, as if someone had kicked it—hard.

"That Waldo is such a rat!" Darius said. "But how can we prove it?"

"We've got to look for evidence the police missed," Delta told him. "It doesn't seem to have occurred to them that the vandal snuck in from the water, so maybe they didn't search that direction."

Delta, Jax, and Darius circled around the crime scene tape and spread out to explore the back border of the cemetery, where the field of grave markers met a hedge of azalea bushes.

"Hey! Over here!" Jax called. "I found a path."

Sure enough, a trail of trampled grasses wove its way through the azaleas and beyond into a thick mass of palmetto shrubs taller than Delta's head. Dragonflies and mosquitos fought for available flight space as the kids headed deeper into the jungled foliage.

"I can't believe I didn't notice this smell when we were here the other night," she said, slapping at a mosquito. She inhaled deeply, relishing the aroma of Carolina pluff mud—the musty, salty combination of living sea marsh and decomposing spartina grasses. When the mud was exposed during low tide, the scent was especially potent. Delta knew that some people hated that smell, but to her, it was heavenly. It meant she was at home in the Sea Islands.

"Check this out," Darius said. He motioned toward a discarded can of spray paint sticking out from beneath a bush on the trail's edge. "It's the same brand we saw on the ferry dock on Daufuskie."

"Right by Waldo's boat," Jax said.

They wound further through the path until they reached the oyster-studded marsh edging Broad Creek. Unlike the wide body of water they had ferried through yesterday, this end of the waterway was only about twenty feet across and heavily wooded on both sides. A dilapidated dock stretched precariously into the creek nearby where an old homestead had apparently once been. Otherwise, no homes were in sight for some distance. It would be easy to slip into this secluded spot unnoticed—especially in the darkness of night.

"He could have tied his boat up to that dock," Darius said. The trio trudged through the thick grasses on the edge of the marsh, careful to stay on solid land. It was easy to sink in wet pluff mud, but often difficult to get back out.

Once on the dock, they stepped cautiously to avoid gaps left by missing boards. The tired old dock sagged toward its end, swaying as the trio's weight challenged it. They stood together in the midday sun, gazing down the length of Broad Creek in the direction of Daufuskie Island.

Darius nodded. "I'd bet anything that this is how Waldo did it."

"It's just like the Tory militia all over again," Jax said.

"Do you think we would've heard Waldo's boat from the cemetery, though?" Delta asked. "It is a powerboat, you know. It wouldn't be as easy to sneak around in as a rowboat."

"He might've gotten here after we left," Darius suggested. "But even if he came while we were here, the sound would have been muffled by all those trees and shrubs we had to walk through."

"And the traffic noise on the road could have drowned it out," Jax said.

"That's right. And he would have driven the last few yards at a really low speed, which isn't that loud," Darius said. "I really think he could have done it without anyone noticing a thing."

Delta placed her hand across her forehead to block the glare as she stared out over the water imagining Tory rowboats—and Waldo's small powerboat—sneaking up the narrowing waterway. Even shielding her eyes from the sun, now high in the October sky, light still blinded her from below somehow. Squinting, she searched the area near her feet and spotted a sparkling dot on the rickety dock. She slowly leaned down to examine the source of the reflection—something small and silver wedged between two weathered wooden boards.

Jax and Darius watched as Delta arose holding a small item between her thumb and index finger. "It looks like a football . . ." she said.

Darius grinned. "It's not just a football. It's the pin the Island High School Sharks wear on their school jackets. They get a new one every year they play on the team."

Darius pulled out his cell phone, tapped it a few times, and held it up for his friends to see. The photo, taken at last weekend's Fall Festival, showed Micah, Jon, and Ivy all wearing their matching jackets.

"See, they all have four pins just like this one."

"Waldo's in their same grade, isn't he?" Delta asked.

"Yep, they're all seniors."

Delta smiled. "Then I'm guessing that, as of last Sunday night, Waldo only has three pins on his jacket."

Jax pumped his fist in the air. "We've got him! The Sea Witch better start laughing, because we're about to get our revenge!"

28

Confronting the Culprit

"If we hurry, we can catch him before he leaves practice," Darius said, pedaling at full speed up the bike path.

To the kids' great luck, Darius had happened to hear Micah and Jon mention yesterday that they had football practice all morning today. Now that Waldo was supposedly replacing Ivy as team kicker, he would definitely be there.

"What are the chances you'd know exactly where Waldo is at this very moment?" Delta said. "We are *meant* to catch him!"

Jax grinned as they rounded the corner toward the high school athletic fields. "He's dead meat for sure."

They pulled around the bleachers of the football arena and saw . . . no one.

"Oh, no! They're already gone," Delta said.

"No, they do their scrimmages over on the practice field," Darius said, pointing across a wide parking lot. The determined trio pedaled quickly across the lot to find that the other field held . . . also no one.

"Man!" Jax said, slapping his handlebars. "I was all ready to get our revenge."

Darius glanced around the parking lot. "I don't think we're too late. There are still a bunch of cars over there by the locker-room doors. Micah says Coach always has a meeting with them after practice, and then they have to shower. Maybe we can catch Waldo heading into the parking lot."

They spotted Micah's old car and parked their bikes behind it. Leaning against the hood, they each took the opportunity to catch their breath. Any time now, their prey was going to step right into the trap they had set for him.

"Here they come!" Jax said as the locker-room doors burst open. A cluster of players entered the parking lot carrying duffle bags and football helmets. Waldo wasn't one of them.

"Let's go closer so we don't miss him," Darius suggested. Delta and Jax followed their friend toward the building, searching the faces of each person passing through the doors.

Jax chuckled. "We really are playing *Where's Waldo?* now!"

Finally, their target stepped outside into the autumn air, his team jacket draped over the duffel bag in his hand.

"Let me do the talking," Darius said as the kids stepped forward.

"Micah's still talking to Coach," Waldo said when he recognized them. "You twerps may have to wait a while."

"We're not waiting for Micah," Jax said. "We're waiting for *you!*"

Delta scowled at her brother. The usually cool-headed Darius was supposed to handle this.

"Why would you be waiting for me?" Waldo smirked.

"Because . . ." Jax's interruption ended when Delta grabbed his arm and squeezed her fingernails into his wrist.

Darius cleared his throat. "We wanted to let you know that your little stunt to get Micah and us into trouble has failed. You've been caught, Waldo."

The teen shrugged. "Hey, man, I just posted the news in the app.

I didn't make it up. If y'all are in trouble, that's your own fault."

"I'm not talking about putting it online," Darius said. "I'm talking about you sneaking up Broad Creek in your boat Sunday night and vandalizing the cemetery. Using the app to blame it on us was just icing on the cake."

Waldo rolled his eyes. "Yeah, right. Like I would waste my time like that on you losers."

"We've got proof," Delta said. She reached into her pocket and pulled out the football pin that would seal Waldo's fate. "We found this on the dock behind Zion Cemetery—right where you lost it."

By this time, several other players had gathered around the group, attracted by the raised voices. They all stared accusingly at Waldo.

Delta and Jax exchanged a grin, reveling in their moment of triumph. Micah would get his scholarship after all! The reputations of Pops and the museum would be cleared, the McGee's restaurant would have customers again, and the kids at school would know that Delta, Jax, and Darius were not criminals. Perhaps most important, Mom and Dad would never have to think that their kids were major screwups.

"You mean, these pins right here?" Waldo asked. He sat his duffel on the ground and lifted his team jacket, holding it up for all to see. Reflected by the October sun, a row of silver pins sparkled on the left-hand chest. A row of *four* pins.

"But . . ." Delta stared at the complete set and then back at the "proof" in her hand. They had been so sure!

"Just because it's not your pin doesn't mean you didn't do it," Jax said.

Waldo laughed. "First of all, idiot, your little piece of 'incriminating evidence' there is useless now that you've removed it from the crime scene. It doesn't mean anything now. Don't y'all watch crime shows on TV?"

Delta's heart sank at the realization that he was probably right. Why hadn't they just called the sheriff when they found the pin? Better yet, they should have told him about their suspicions and the possibility of someone sneaking into the cemetery from Broad Creek. Then the sheriff's department could have done its job.

"And not that I owe you any explanations," Waldo continued, "but I happen to have a rock-solid alibi for last Sunday night."

"You do?" Darius asked.

"That's right. I was on duty at the Daufuskie Volunteer Fire Department all night long. There were three other firefighters there with me. You can ask any of them."

"Oh." Darius stared at his feet as the other players laughed and scattered through the parking lot. Delta still held the now-useless pin in her hand, and Jax looked about ready to cry.

"Nice try," Waldo said over his shoulder as he headed toward a friend's car with his gear.

"I really thought it was him," Delta said. "I mean, all the pieces fit."

Darius nodded. "None of our suspects have panned out. Now we're back to square one."

Sighing, Delta lifted the little silver football to the sun. She twitched it back and forth, allowing the reflected light to dance in the branches of a tree edging the parking lot.

"What are y'all doing here?"

Delta looked up to see Micah approaching them. Suddenly, his eyes grew wide, and a smile spread across his face as he recognized the item she was holding.

"Hey! You found Jon's missing pin!" he said. "He's been looking for that thing all week."

29

Facing the Truth

"Hey, look, Jon!" Micah called across the parking lot. "Delta found that pin you lost!"

Delta, Jax, and Darius stared across to where Jon was exiting the building. He approached the group with a smile.

"Cool! Was it here in the parking lot?" he asked.

"Um, no," Delta said, glancing at Darius and Jax. "We found it at the Zion Cemetery."

"Huh," Jon said, his brow furrowed. "It must have dropped off my jacket when we were there last Saturday for the Fall Festival."

Jax shook his head. "No, you still had the pin then."

"How would you know that?" Micah asked.

"Show them the picture, Darius," Jax said.

Darius slipped his phone from his pocket and pulled up the photo he had taken at the Island History Museum last Saturday night. He held it out so Micah and Jon could see.

"Remember? Y'all had just come back from 'Ghostly Tales,' and we took some pictures of your costumes. You have all four of your pins in this photo, Jon."

"Well, you told me on Monday that you'd lost one," Micah said, so it must have happened on Sunday."

"But he didn't come with us to the cemetery on Sunday," Delta said. Jon's face reddened.

"Oh, that's right!" he said finally. "I forgot that I stopped by the cemetery on Sunday afternoon."

"What for?" Micah asked.

"I thought I might have dropped my cell phone there, but then I found it in my jacket pocket." He shrugged and laughed nervously.

"So, where did you look for your phone at the cemetery?" Darius asked him.

Jon shrugged. "Geez, I don't know. Like, by the tombstones, where we were telling our stories at the festival. What's with all the questions?"

"It's just that we found the pin somewhere else," Delta said. "It was stuck between a couple of boards on the dock *behind* the cemetery."

"Dock? What dock?" Micah asked.

"Zion backs right up to Broad Creek," Darius told him. "You have to go through a bunch of bushes and stuff, but there's a path directly from the cemetery to an old dock. That's where we found Jon's pin."

"And there was a can of orange spray paint along the path, too," Jax said. "The same brand we saw by the ferry terminal on Daufuskie." Delta had forgotten that piece of evidence.

"We thought Waldo took the paint from Daufuskie and snuck up Broad Creek to the cemetery in his boat," she said.

Micah frowned. "Waldo? You thought he did all that damage at Zion?"

"Sure! I bet that's what happened!" Jon said. "He can be a real jerk."

"Except that *isn't* what happened," Delta said, "because he has an alibi, and the pin wasn't his. It's *your* pin, Jon."

The teen scowled and took the pin from Delta, examining it. "Maybe this isn't mine, after all," he said. "Everybody on the team has them. It could be anyone's."

"You could have taken one of your family's boats from Daufuskie up Broad Creek," Jax said. "You could have taken a can of paint from the dock."

"But why would he do that?" Micah said. "Jon and I are best friends. Why would he want to get us all in so much trouble?"

They all looked at Jon, his face flushed, tears welling in his eyes.

"You didn't do that, did you?" Micah said.

"It was supposed to be a joke," Jon said, so softly they could barely hear him.

Micah stared at his friend. "What are you saying?"

"My dad was supposed to watch the Falcons game on TV with me Sunday night, but then he bagged, as usual. Some work thing came up." Jon sniffed and wiped his eyes. "So, I figured maybe I could catch up with you and Ivy at the cemetery. I'd grabbed a can of that paint from the dock. They're marking the ground for a new cable network or something, so that paint's sitting around everywhere."

"And . . ." Micah prompted.

"I wasn't going to paint anything," Jon said. "I was just going to sneak up on you and shake the can. You know how it makes a rattling noise, like a snake, when you shake a can of spray paint? I thought it might freak you out. It was supposed to be funny."

"So, what happened?" Micah asked.

Jon sighed. "I came creeping up from the creek, but you had already left by the time I got there. I was mad that I missed hanging out with y'all, and mad at my dad for never being around. I was just angry, so I kicked a tombstone. It fell over, which made me even madder, but also felt kind of good. So, I kicked some more, and an old fence, too."

"What about the paint?" Delta asked.

Jon shrugged. "I still had the can in my hand, and I almost threw it in the bushes. But then I noticed the mausoleum and I just started spraying on it. I don't know why I put the team's name on there, but then it occurred to me that I may have given myself away by doing that."

"So, you added my initials," Micah said.

Jon looked at his feet and nodded. When he lifted his head, tears were streaming down his face. "I'm so sorry, Micah! I had no idea it'd cause so much trouble! Everybody sees you as this *golden boy*, so I figured you'd get off with maybe a hand slap. Even my own dad thinks you walk on water! Ever since you and I trained with that pro, Dad's always saying he wishes I had your 'natural talent.' I mean, I play in the same games you do, and I do all the same volunteer stuff as you, but *you're* the 'Good Citizen Athlete.' I guess I thought you could survive a little bad press. I didn't even think about the possibility of you losing your scholarship."

"Any trouble here?"

Delta looked up to see the football coach approaching them, a concerned frown on his face. Jon swiped his hand over his wet cheeks and turned to the man.

"Some trouble, yeah," he said. "But maybe you can help me make it right, Coach. Would you go with me to talk to the sheriff?"

"I can't wait until Mom and Dad call!" Jax said. "Now they'll know we're not criminals!"

Tootsie and Pops walked the sheriff to the front door of their house and waved goodbye. This had been an especially welcomed visit, as he had officially declared the kids no longer suspects in the Zion Cemetery vandalism. Coach had escorted Jon to the sheriff's office earlier to make his statement and turn himself in as the actual perpetrator.

"I never believed you kiddos were criminals, you know," Pops said.

"But sometimes even good kids make bad decisions."

"Like Jon?" Jax asked.

Pops nodded. "That's a perfect example."

"What's going to happen to him now?" Delta asked. "Will he go to jail?"

"I'll bet Micah's so mad!" Jax said. "He'll want Jon to be put away for a long time for what he did."

"We'll have to wait and see," Pops replied. "He's still seventeen, so that may help."

"Hopefully Micah will get his scholarship now," Tootsie said.

"Yeah," Delta agreed, "but I still feel awful for him. His best friend totally betrayed him!"

The family sat in silence for a few moments, pondering the turn of events.

Suddenly, Pops snapped his fingers. "I have an idea! How about we do a little cemetery cleanup tomorrow?"

"I don't know, Pops," Delta said. "I'm not sure we're supposed to go over there anymore."

"I'll make some calls and get permission," he said. "They'll be hiring professionals to repair the damage Jon did, but Zion could use some general sprucing up, too. You know, pulling weeds, trimming overgrown brush, replacing faded flags and flowers. That sort of thing."

"But why do *we* have to do it?" Jax whined. "We've been found innocent."

"That's just the point, Jackson. You don't *have* to do it. Let's do it just because it's a nice thing to do."

30

Changing the History

Delta was standing on the front lawn of the Island History Museum singing "God Save the Queen" as her brother hoisted a British flag on the museum's flagpole. Next to her, Pops stood sporting a white powdered wig. Her grandmother approached carrying a silver tray laden with a porcelain teapot and a plate of scones.

"'Ello, guvnah!" Tootsie said.

"Wake up, Delta! The magic is gone!"

Delta opened her eyes to find herself in bed, Jax leaning over her clutching the new-and-ruined Crazy Box.

"I left a purple and white oyster shell as a gift for Mercy last night before I went to bed," he said, "but there is still no journal. What if the magic is really gone, and what if it stopped before she even saw our warning?"

Delta sat up. *Or what if Mercy did see our message, and whatever she did about it changed everything? What if altering that one battle changed the war, and that affected the whole future of our country? What if we caused the British to win the Revolutionary War, just like in my dream?*

"It's too late now," Delta said. "We'll just have to wait and see."

The family was hard at work at the Zion Cemetery, determined to do their part to beautify the historic site. Pops had gained approval from the city council and declared the areas near the yellow tape strictly off-limits, so no trouble should come from this outing.

Tootsie was busy replacing worn flower bouquets with fresh ones on the graves, while Pops tackled a vine that had infiltrated the azalea bushes lining the graveyard. Meanwhile, the kids were filling paper grocery sacks with weeds poking up among the tombstones.

"Look at that!" Jax whispered, nodding toward the overgrown foliage near the back of the cemetery. "The Sea Witch has come to say hi."

Near the pathway to the marsh, a bright orange fox sat gazing in their direction. After a few seconds of shared silence, it stood and, with a twitch of its tail, disappeared down the trail.

Jax raced after the animal, while Delta stopped at the spot where it had been sitting. At the base of a cluster of ferns, she spied a chunk of white rock. Kneeling, she pushed back the plants to find that what she had seen was actually the tip of a larger flat stone with an embossed metal placard on its surface. Bold lettering spanning the monument read: *Charles Davant, Pvt. S.C. Militia.*

"Jax! You've got to see this!" she called.

Her brother trudged back up the path. "I couldn't catch it."

"Who cares? I uncovered Mercy's father's tombstone!"

Jax knelt behind her, and they read the rest of the previously hidden tribute.

"It says he was mortally wounded by members of the Royal Militia of Daufuskie on October 22, 1781. He's considered a hero of the Revolution because he warned all the other members of the Patriot

Militia to save them from the attack."

"It says that, because of the bravery of Charles Davant, he was 'the only known Patriot casualty on the island.'" Jax said. "Does that mean he was the only one who died?"

Delta nodded.

"But I thought the whole militia was killed?" Jax said.

"Not anymore," Delta said. "Mercy got our warning."

"What's that you found?" Pops asked, leaning over his grandkids. The kids sat back so he could see.

"It's a tombstone for a guy named Charles Davant," Delta said. "It says he was a local hero during the Revolutionary War."

"I'll say he was!" Pops said, kneeling down to read the placard fully.

"So, you've actually heard of this guy?" Jax asked.

"Of course!" Pops said. "What happened is, the Patriot Militia was supposed to meet that night, but Davant got word somehow that the militia from Daufuskie were going to ambush them. Davant went to the Muster House early and warned everyone who showed up to leave. By the time the Tories arrived, he was the only Patriot left."

"But he still died," Delta said.

Pops nodded. "Yes, but he gave his life to save his fellow Patriots."

Without warning, Pops grabbed a fern plant and pulled it up by its roots. "This stone should never have been covered up," he said. "I'll clear the area and suggest to the city council that a fence be erected around it. Everyone on the island should know this history."

This history, Delta thought. Had she and Jax actually changed the past?

Things got even weirder when the family stopped at the Island History Museum on the way home. While Pops picked up some papers in his office, Tootsie was deep in conversation with a volunteer in the museum bookstore.

"I want to look at something," Delta told her brother. He followed her down the hallway and to the *Muster House Massacre* shadowbox.

"What the heck?" Jax said.

Instead of recounting a massacre, the display was now headlined *Death of a Hero/Birth of the Bloody Legion*. The map of the area was still the same, but the story described was significantly different.

"This matches Pops's story about Charles Davant, except it says he was 'warned by his eleven-year-old daughter of the impending ambush.'"

"That would be Mercy!" Jax said.

Delta nodded. "Apparently, her dad was able to ride back to Two Oaks, but he collapsed in the arms of his wife before dying. His last words were, 'Get Martinangel!'"

"Like, Philip Martinangel?" Jax asked. "Mrs. Talbird's brother-in-law?"

"Yes, and then the Bloody Legion part happened."

"Ooh! What's that?" Jax asked.

"This says that, not long after Davant was shot, the Patriot militia on Hilton Head decided to retaliate by sneaking over to Daufuskie. They crept into Martinangel's house in the middle of the night and slit his throat while he was sleeping in his bed. After that, our militia here was known as 'the Bloody Legion.'"

"Awesome!"

"It is *not* awesome, Jax! Don't you get it? Everyone wanted revenge, so the suffering just kept going back and forth. First, the Patriots killed someone, so the Tories burned their houses. Next, the Patriots planned to get even for that attack, but the Tories had to avenge that by killing Charles Davant."

"And then the Patriots had to get revenge for his death by killing Martinangel."

"Exactly." Delta sighed. "It's a wonder it ever stopped at all."

"Oh, good. You found it," Pops said. "I was hoping to show you kiddos this display after you found that marker at the cemetery."

Delta stepped aside so her grandfather could see the exhibit, too.

"When did you change this?" she asked.

"What do you mean?" Pops replied. "This display has been here for years. I'm surprised you hadn't noticed it before. I always thought the boat model was a neat feature."

Delta and Jax looked again at the wooden model of a flat-bottomed rowboat, just as they'd seen a couple of days ago. But the opened book next to it was definitely a new addition to the shadowbox.

"How'd that journal get in there?" Jax asked.

"We inserted it when we built the display," Pops explained. "I should probably open it back up and dust it one of these days."

"Stop kidding, Pops," Delta said. "That's why we haven't seen Mercy's journal for a couple of days. You put it in your exhibit!"

Pops frowned. "What? Like I told you, this exhibit has been here—just like it is—for at least four or five years. There's no need to update it." He chuckled. "It's not like history is going to change!"

A museum visitor stopped to ask Pops a question, so Delta and Jax leaned over to study the familiar antique journal in the shadow box. The paper was still smooth and the delicate, familiar handwriting clear. Once again, Delta wished she could read cursive, but she could make out some things.

"The date on this entry is 12 February 1796. That's nearly fifteen years after her father died."

"So, Mercy kept writing in her journal, even after we stopped reading it," Jax said.

"I'm going to try something," Delta said, standing. She pulled her phone from her pocket and typed onto the screen *Mercy Abigail Davant*.

Looking over her shoulder, Jax said, "You're not going to find anything. Remember? You already searched."

"But things have changed now, Jax. Listen to this: 'The daughter of Revolutionary War hero Charles Davant, Mercy Abigail Davant Pinkney changed agriculture in the colonial Carolinas by developing a special blend of Sea Island cotton that became one of its most important cash crops. Manager of three plantations, Mrs. Pinkney had a major influence on the colonial economy.'"

"So, now we know what happened to her!" Jax said.

"We know what happened to her *now*," Delta corrected. "In the version where we didn't warn her, who knows what became of Mercy Davant?"

"We really changed history, didn't we, Delta?"

"You know something, Jax? I think we really did."

31

Breaking the Cycle

A chilly breeze blew off of Port Royal Sound as the Veteran's Day Tribute was held at the ruins of Hilton Head's historic Fort Walker. Pops had been pleased when the Island History Museum and local Veterans of Foreign Wars chapter were granted permission by the city council to hold the celebration there. A couple of weeks had passed since Jon admitted his guilt in the cemetery vandalism and—for everyone but Jon—life was pretty much back to normal.

Delta glanced overhead and appreciated the American flags— not British—that fluttered in the November sky. Thankfully, the "new history" their warning had created had apparently not caused significant changes to their world. She glanced around her at the ruins of Fort Walker, perched on a bluff at the northern tip of the island. Overlooking Port Royal Sound and the Atlantic Ocean beyond, this was the location of the only Civil War battle fought on Hilton Head Island. The Union Army's victory here had changed the course of the war. The slaves on the island had been the first in the nation to live freely, working toward lives as independent Americans. At least one of them, Delta knew, was Darius's and Micah's ancestor.

Delta, Jax, and Darius stood near the front of the crowd as Micah prepared to accept his "Good Citizen" scholarship. Thankfully, the VFW had been quick to apologize to Micah and reinstate his award once they learned of his true innocence in the Zion matter.

"Look who had the nerve to show his face here," Jax said, motioning toward a man and a teenage boy approaching the stage.

"No way! They're not still giving Jon an award, are they?"

Darius shook his head. "No, the VFW took that away right before they gave Micah's scholarship back."

"Then why is Jon here, and who's that with him?" Jax asked.

"That's his dad," Darius said. "Micah said Jon and his dad are trying to spend more time together these days."

"Before he goes to jail, you mean?"

"No, Jax. He's not going to jail," Darius said. "He's got to do community service for the rest of forever, though. And he had to pay a big fine, too."

"His family won't even miss that money," Jax said. "I'll bet Micah's mad Jon didn't get punished worse than that."

"Actually, he's not," Darius said. "In fact, he invited Jon and his dad to come here today. They're joining our family for lunch at the Geechee Grill afterwards, too."

"Really?" Delta said. "I wouldn't blame Micah if he never wanted to see Jon again."

"I asked him about that," Darius said. "He and Jon have been best friends since they were little kids, and Micah doesn't want to give up on that. He said forgiving Jon is a process, but one he's willing to work on."

"Wow," Jax said. "He didn't want revenge for what Jon put him through?"

"Nope. He said revenge just keeps pain moving. He'd rather try to forgive Jon and move on."

Delta thought again of the horrible game of revenge played by the Patriots and Tories of the Sea Islands. She thought of the Sea Witch, who was said to forever seek revenge for a wrong done to her, and the Yemassees and Daufuskie islanders who took turns killing each other on Bloody Point. Did their vengeance bring them peace? She doubted that it did.

Micah walked across the stage and accepted an oversized fake check from the VFW to denote his college tuition. After thanking the uniformed man presenting him with the honor, the teen smiled and waved to the audience. Delta saw him nod to Jon, who was clapping and whistling for his accomplished friend.

Yes, Micah had chosen a better way.

Darius, Delta, and Jax strolled toward a series of historical markers describing the battle of Port Royal Sound which had taken place on this very site.

"I still can't believe y'all managed to change history," Darius said.

Jax shook his head. "I know. Isn't it wild?"

"I'm not even sure I'm glad we did it," Delta said. "I mean, saving all those militia men was good, and Mercy grew up to have a successful life, but we caused some bad stuff to happen, too. Even though her father became a hero, he still died. And Philip Martinangel was killed by the Bloody Legion, which didn't happen at all until we warned Mercy."

"Well, I'm just glad you didn't upset the natural universe or something," Darius told his friends. "By changing the past for Mercy, you could have created a whole different future for us."

"There you kiddos are," Pops said as he and Tootsie joined the kids. "It's been a great celebration, but now we need to head to the airport."

"Are we going somewhere?" Jax asked.

Pops chuckled. "We've got to pick up Carly. Remember? She's visiting from college. It's been on the calendar for weeks."

"Who's Carly?" Delta asked.

This time, Tootsie laughed. "Very funny!"

"No, seriously," Jax said. "Who's Carly?"

Pops and Tootsie looked at each other and shook their heads.

"Your big sister, Carly, that's who," Tootsie said. "What other Carly would I be talking about, silly?"

As their grandparents headed toward the parking lot, Delta and Jax stared blankly after them.

"You never told me you have an older sister," Darius said to his friends.

"That's because we *don't*," Delta told him.

Darius smiled. "You mean, you *didn't*."

Delta and Jax exchanged a wide-eyed stare, and then he raised his arms in the air and smiled.

"Welcome to the new future!" he said. "Let's go meet our sister!"

Fact or Fiction?

Even though *The Sea Witch's Revenge* is a fictional novel and Delta and her family and friends are inventions of the author, many of the places, people, and events in the story are based in fact.

 Hilton Head and Daufuskie are both real South Carolina Sea Islands. Although bitter enemies during the Revolutionary War, the islands' residents are quite friendly to one another today. While Hilton Head Island is accessible by bridge, you can visit Daufuskie Island via a ferry ride just as Delta, Jax, and their friends did.

 Although Mercy Davant is a fictional character, her father, Charles Davant, is a real historical figure. He was the owner of Two Oaks Plantation on Hilton Head Island and served in the Hilton Head Patriot Militia. As in the "new history" created by Delta and Jax, Charles Davant was killed by Tories from Daufuskie Island near the Muster House on October 22, 1781. As he lay dying in his wife's arms, his last words were: "Get Martinangel!"

Just like in the "new history," a militia group from Hilton Head did avenge Davant's murder by sneaking to Daufuskie Island and killing Philip Martinangel. A newspaper in Charleston, South Carolina, reported the attack and called the Hilton Head militia "the Bloody Legion"—a name that has been used to describe them ever since.

 The Zion Cemetery really exists and is currently owned and maintained by the Heritage Library of Hilton Head. You can visit the historic site to see the Baynard Mausoleum and the graves of many significant figures in the island's past, including that of Charles Davant, who really was the only Patriot killed on Hilton Head during the Revolutionary War.

 Francis "Swamp Fox" Marion is a real Patriot hero of the Revolutionary War. It is well documented that some men from Hilton Head Island (including John Talbird, Mary Ann Talbird's husband) served with him as one of "Marion's Men." In one of those skirmishes, Talbird was captured by the British and imprisoned on a ship in Charleston Harbor, just as described in *The Sea Witch's Revenge*. Although there is no record that Francis Marion ever personally visited Hilton Head, there is also no record stating that he did *not* visit the island. So, maybe . . .

 The story of the Talbird Oak is true. Baby Henry "Yorktown" Talbird received that nickname later because he was born on the same day that General Charles Cornwallis surrendered to General George Washington at Yorktown. You can still visit the historic Talbird Oak just inside the back entrance to Hilton Head Plantation.

Delta and Jax ask Darius how it makes him feel to know that some of his ancestors were slaves. Since the author is not Gullah-Geechee herself, she consulted with members of the Gullah community to compose Darius' response to his friends. If you were Darius, how would you have answered that question?

 Constance "Sea Witch" True and her sad tale are purely creations of the author. However, hundreds of innocent people in the American Colonies were accused of witchcraft in the late 1600s and early 1700s. Most of those found guilty were women and teenage girls who were considered unruly or "different" in some way, such as knowing how to heal with herbal medicines. This was especially common in the New England area, most famously in Salem, Massachusetts.

 Although Pops is a fictional character, his Island History Museum is based on Hilton Head's very real Coastal Discovery Museum, an affiliate of the Smithsonian Institute. As in *The Sea Witch's Revenge*, this facility offers indoor and outdoor exhibits, classes, and special events throughout the year. Check it out at www.coastaldiscovery.org.

Acknowledgments

A novel is the creation of far more than the author named on the book's cover. Primarily, *The Sea Witch's Revenge* would not exist without the consistent encouragement of loyal readers—young and older—who kept asking for Delta's and Jax's next adventure. I offer great thanks to the good folks at Koehler Books, my cohorts in the Island Writers Network, Jonathan Haupt and the rest of the crew at the Pat Conroy Literary Center, and Sally Sue Lavigne of the charming Storybook Shoppe in Bluffton, SC. Huge appreciation to my trusty sounding board and diehard supporter Dina Massachi. So much love to Kelly, Brad, Kyla, Hannah, and Mike, who have been such good sports about adopting Delta, Jax, and Darius into our family. Hugs to my darling grandbabies, who inspire me to tell more stories for them to someday read. And last—but never, ever least—the greatest love of all to my partner and muse, Steve. You are my past, my present, and my always.

ALSO BY

SUSAN DIAMOND RILEY

The Sea Island's Secret: A Delta & Jax Mystery

The Sea Turtle's Curse: A Delta & Jax Mystery

CPSIA information can be obtained
at www.ICGtesting.com
Printed in the USA
LVHW112147121222
735105LV00030B/602

9 781646 637904